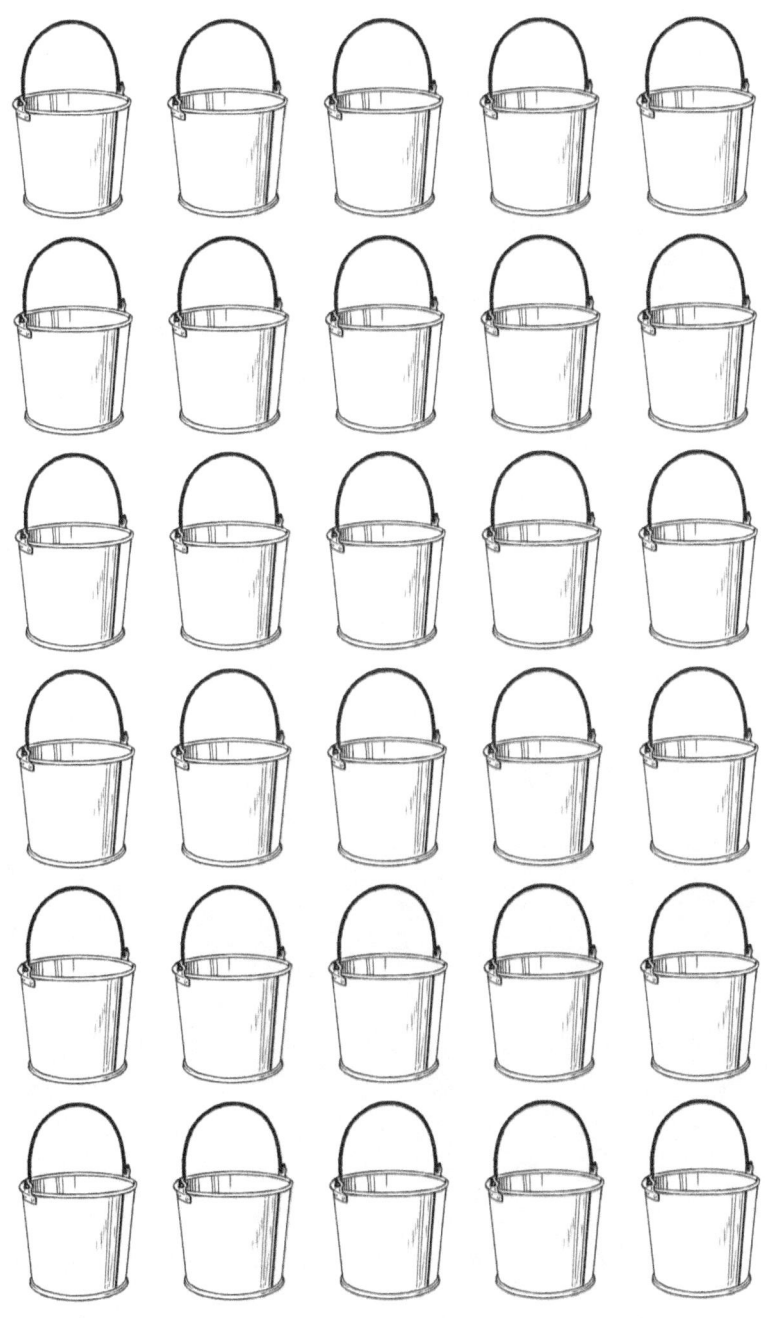

Pure Slush Books

Part Sloan Books

2014

September

Vol. 9

a Pure Slush book

Pure Slush

2014 September Vol. 9 is edited by Matt Potter and
published by Pure Slush, June 2014.

All stories are copyright © the individual authors

Original cover photograph copyright © Cecilia Johansson
Front cover design by Matt Potter

ISBN: 978-1-925101-43-0

Find *Pure Slush* at http://pureslush.webs.com

Copies of all *Pure Slush* publications can be bought
at http://pureslush.webs.com/store.htm

All queries re *Pure Slush* can be made
via email to edpureslush@live.com.au

A note on differences in punctuation and spelling

Pure Slush proudly features (both online and in print) writers from all over the English-speaking world. Some speak and write English as their first language, while for others, it's their second or third or even fourth language. Naturally, across all versions of English, there are differences in punctuation and spelling, and even in meaning. These differences are reflected in the stories *Pure Slush* publishes, and it accounts for any differences in punctuation, spelling and meaning found within these pages.

stories by

Guilie Castillo-Oriard	James Claffey
Townsend Walker	Gwendolyn Joyce Mintz
Derek Osborne	Stephen V. Ramey
Gloria Garfunkel	Gay Degani
John Wentworth Chapin	Sally-Anne Macomber
Lynn Beighley	Mandy Nicol
Andrew Stancek	Margaret Bingel
Rachel Ambrose	Darryl Price
Gill Hoffs	Teresa Burns Gunther
Susan Tepper	Matt Potter
Jessica McHugh	Gary Percesepe
Shane Simmons	Nathaniel Tower
Michelle Elvy	Kimberlee Smith
Len Kuntz	Vanessa Weibler Paris
Michael Webb	Joanne Jagoda

The Bonaire Feel-Good

by Guilie Castillo-Oriard

There's a new bounce in Luis Villalobos's step this Monday morning. He takes the sweeping stairs to the Ehrlich Fiduciary building two by two and dances a Rocky Balboa victory hop, face lifted up to the morning sun, at the summit. The wind in his ears could be the roar of an adoring crowd.

The receptionist pushes one half of the glass doors open for him. Was she watching? Well, what if she was? He gives her a big smile. "Bon día, Rochandra." He's making an effort with Papiamentu, now that he has a private tutor. Of sorts.

Rochandra looks him up and down. "Bon dia i bon siman."

Bon siman. He always forgets that on Mondays. Not just *good morning* but also *good week.* What a lovely custom. He's never seen it anywhere else; maybe it's unique to Curaçao.

Curaçao. He came so close to leaving without giving this island a chance. He'd have missed so much. His dog Al, for instance. And Pélagie.

"There's a package for you." Rochandra brandishes a clipboard. "Will you sign for it now, or shall I send the messenger up later?"

"Now's fine. Danki."

She hauls a FedEx box onto the counter and hands him the clipboard. "Had a good weekend?"

He scans the spreadsheet of incoming correspondence for his name. "More than good, actually."

Rochandra is leaning on the counter, the picture of an eager fifth-grade gossip – notwithstanding the gray hair and the fact she weighs roughly four times the average fifth-grader. "What did you do?"

"I, uh … I went to Bonaire."

"Bonaire?" Maybe it's the way he hesitated, or the way his gaze slid away from hers, but Rochandra is looking like a hyena that's just spotted a wounded gazelle all alone in the savannah. "I never pegged you for a lover of peace and quiet. Why would you go to Bonaire?"

"Well, I –"

"Oh, you're a diver! I forgot, yes. And? You loved it, no?"

"Yes, it's –"

"Your dog must've missed you. Poor thing, left all alone."

Normally, Luis finds Curaçao's corporate informality refreshing. Right now, though, he's missing the distance that deference provides. It's unsettling that a receptionist should know so much about his life. "He went with me. Sorry, I can't find where I'm supposed to sign."

He pushes the clipboard back to her, but she doesn't even notice. She's staring at him, quite literally agape. "You took your *dog* to Bonaire?"

He forces a smile. "Rochandra. Where do I need to sign?"

She lifts an eyebrow, miffed but not chastised, and flips with exaggerated gestures to another page. "Right *here*. Where your *name* is."

When he's Managing Director – the announcement should be made any day now – he'll hire a new receptionist.

As he hands the clipboard back, something catches his eye. "Is this date right? This package came in on Thursday?"

She barely glances at the page. "If that's what the manifest says."

The package most likely contains incorporation documents – which might've generated immediately collectible revenue if delivered last week. No point in belaboring the issue; not today, not with this attitude. He thanks her again, doesn't get a reply.

His Bonaire feel-good is fading fast.

He'll bring up the mailroom at the Efficiency Development Team meeting. He rescheduled it for today; he and Al had to meet Pélagie at the airport at three on Friday, so he took the afternoon off. First time he's done that since he arrived in Curaçao back in December. But it's Labor Day today. US banks will be closed. Plenty of time to catch up.

His phone rings as he walks to the elevator. Fifty bucks – fifty thousand – say it's Milena again. He expected a big scene and put off telling her about Pélagie longer than he should have, but she's been surprisingly mature about the whole thing. Until Saturday, when she lost it. Forty-three missed calls over the weekend. Voice mail, texts, even emails asking, pleading, then finally demanding he call her back, all of which greeted him this morning when the plane landed and Pélagie returned the Blackberry she confiscated on Friday. That was the deal: no expectations, no cheesiness, no Ehrlich. *The financial world does revolve without you*, she said.

For an adrenaline-soaked moment at the airport, the calls panicked Luis. But knowing Milena, it's either plain jealousy – somehow she found out he was with Pélagie – or more bullshit about the MD announcement. She's theatrical, wants it to come off all Cirque de Soleil. Useless, and moot; everyone already knows the job is his. But she's still MD now. He'll drop off his things in his office and go find her, make some sort of amends.

The elevator arrives with a muted ding. Before the doors open, he hears Rochandra's internal line buzzing and her voice, sans the mood, when she answers. "Bon dia, dushi. Oh, he just – he's going up now. But – he's already in the elevator. I can't –"

It's got to be Milena. Luis calls out, "Someone looking for me?"

He hears the clack of the receiver being returned to its cradle before she replies. "No. No one."

Could he have misunderstood? No; there's no one else here. This is bordering on insubordination. Anywhere else in the world he'd call her on it, but Curaçao has quirky labor laws. He's watched Milena jump through the most unreasonable hoops to avoid employment litigation. Best to take it up with HR first.

Goodbye, Bonaire feel-good.

But he'll be back. Pélagie goes at least once a month to check on the shelter there. He's pretty sure he earned a standing invitation after his performance this weekend. He catches his own eye in the elevator mirror. *Tiger.*

No, it's not the sex. It was good, *he* was good, which doesn't always happen when he's that into someone; he seems to do best on casual between-the-sheets encounters. Less pressure, maybe. Lower stakes. Not that this – this *thing* with Pélagie is going anywhere. She's been very clear, if not very vocal: she has no inclination for romantic entanglements. He senses an old hurt there; he's an idiot for not leaving it alone. But she says it's all about the now. You, me, here, why not. She's big on the fact of coincidence, not its significance.

The self-serving ego-trip junkie in him insists she's right.

He committed to the MD job here for two years; spending even just a fraction of that time with Pélagie will make it not just bearable but memorable. And after …

Well. She knows he's leaving. It's not like he's lied, or made any kind of *promises* –

The elevator doors slide open to Wendolyn's smile. A frantic sort of smile.

"Morning. Not good, by the looks of you. What's wrong?"

"Wrong? Nothing!" Her voice is pitched higher than usual, and her grip, as she takes hold of his arm, feels jittery. "But there's, uh, something I need you to look at. It's on my desk."

"I'll be right there. Let me leave this in my –"

"Do that after. Super urgent, uh, loan agreement. The bank's waiting."

She's tugging on his arm, which had a better chance of working without the backdrop of Rochandra's cheekiness. "They can wait ten seconds more," he says.

"Please! It's –"

And then he hears the shouting. Milena, from the direction of his office. The direction Wendolyn seems bent on keeping him away from. The grip of her hand is so tight his shirt is wrinkling. "Wendolyn? What's going on?"

She says something, but he's already moving past her towards the sound of Milena in full-blown rage.

"I don't care if the email came from GOD HIMSELF! Take this shit down *now*! How dare you, how FUCKING –"

Luis comes around the corner and the scene freezes into a diorama. Josinelle, Stepan's elderly assistant, cowering just inside the door to Stepan's office and clutching, incongruously, a bouquet of red balloons. Behind her, even more incongruously, Stepan himself standing on his desk, next to the dangling half of a CONGRATULATIONS banner. The other half is still taped to the top of the window frame. More red balloons, still tied together in threes, litter the floor under him. The new legal intern, whose name Luis can't remember – has he even met her? she looks completely unfamiliar, but then so does

17

everything else right now – stands by the whiteboard on the opposite wall. Someone spent a valuable chunk of time drawing a two-tone poster on it, which the intern is – was – erasing. Only the lower right corner remains; a too-large exclamation mark surrounded by childishly cute stars and pointillist umbrellas that Luis assumes represent fireworks. It must've been drawn a day ago, at least, because the ghost of the foot-high letters is still all too visible.

Congrats, new MD!
You deserve it!

Milena stares at him from the doorway, fury melting like butter on a griddle. "Why the bloody fuck didn't you return my calls?"

La Ronde /
Sal and Lana

by Townsend Walker

Sal's been calling back to New York to get in touch with Dmitri Ivanovich about this hit job. Dmitri did a couple of things for him earlier in the year, but the last job was botched badly. Supposed to hit the guy in the knee cap, cripple him for good, broke his leg instead, clean break and now the guy is up, walking, and got such religion from his physical therapist that he's entered the New York Marathon.

So Dmitri owes Sal big time. Sal figures with this much ownage he can get D-Man to do the job on this Wall Street guy for peanuts – south side of 20K – and pocket the rest of the 250K. He'll get back what he lost to that dumb ass producer Jimmie Farley. What a flake. He can't believe he fell for the pitch. Last time.

Dmitri hasn't been answering his phone. Goes to voice mail, then, *This mail box is full. Call later.* Middle of all this Sal got a call from his mother in Queens. "Salvatore, caro, your papa's not doing so good. He wants he should see you one last time."

"My Papa wants to see me? See me? You gotta be kidding. Twenty years ago he said *Get out of my life, I don't want your shadow to cross my face, even after I'm dead and don't know it.*"

"Mio figlio, he's dying. He's thinking, maybe he was too hard on you. You were young, a bit wild, no?"

"Yeah, but I still don't want to see him."

"For me, Salvatore, for me. Come for me, your Mama. I want him to die in peace."

"Okay, I come for you, not for him, for you, and I make nice."

Plus Sal can check up on Dmitri, nail that sucker. Get him to do the job while he's there and collect from the Park Avenue dame.

Sal got on the plane yesterday morning and landed at JFK last night. He's staying in Manhattan. See the old man, sure; sleep in the same house, not gonna happen. Hit the hotel bar, had a few, stayed late watching a shimmery jazz singer; so this morning he's getting up slowly and late and the green sequins scattered on the bed shining in the morning sun are hurting his eyes. He rolls over and a sequin digs into his butt. *Shit.* He's awake; he remembers to call Dmitri. No, first coffee, then Dmitri.

A woman answers, lilting English accent. Sal stumbles a "Sorry, I misdialed;" checks the number; dials again, same accented woman's voice. "I was looking for Dmitri Ivanovich. This was his phone, sorry for the trouble."

"It is Dmitri's phone, or was. I'm his sister, Lana Cameron."

"Was? You said was?"

"Indisposed, as they say. Rather permanently, I fear."

"What happened?"

"Something we're not at liberty to speak about."

Her voice is quickly charming Sal into indiscretion.

"I had some work for him."

"I've taken over some of his affairs. Perhaps I can be of assistance."

Sal's thinking: voice like this, I'd like to see the rest of her. He arranges to meet at two in Astoria Park on one of the benches facing Ditmans Boulevard, near the clump of trees.

"I'll be waiting – grey / brown suit, blond hair."

"Me – jeans, heels, also blond, I'm thinking longer than yours."

Sal visits his father who, thankfully, is asleep. He sits by the bed next to his mother for an hour, squeezes his father's hand, "Take care Papa," kisses his mother and restrains himself from running out the door.

At 1:45 he's on the bench in the Park watching passersby. The September sun is still warm and there's a pale breeze off the river. He misses this part of the year back here. California is too same-ol' sometimes. A cluster of people, looking like they all got off the bus together. A blonde emerges; she looks around at the benches, nods towards him and strides across the lawn. This is Lana, oh my god. At least six feet tall, the long hair, peasant blouse (filled out), painted-on jeans, turned up cuffs, silver ankle bangles and five inch heels. She stretches out her hand; the wide red mouth is smiling a welcome, the icy blue eyes are not.

"I say, I wasn't sure what to expect from a Salvatore Mancuso. I'm pleasantly surprised."

Sal, momentarily nonplused, stumbles through something complimentary without saying what he is obviously thinking. *Would this be good in bed, or what?*

"So, tell me about Dmitri."

"A vow of silence there, I'm afraid. I can reveal that I understand why you may have phoned him."

"You're his sister? Him, I could hardly understand. You speak English better than me. And the name, Lana? Is that Russian?"

"Svetlana, Lana. Spent time in London, attached to the Embassy. You've heard of FSB, successor to KGB? Doing a spot of freelance now."

"So you know about all of this, what Dmitri was doing? What to do? How to do it?"

"Trained by the best."

She brings her hands up and puts them around his face, pulls it toward hers. He's thinking, *what kind of game is this? Okay, play along.* She stops an inch away and whispers, "Who, where, when, how and how much?"

He likes this attitude in business. Sal relaxes; he's found his hit girl and she's hungry. He tells her what he knows about a woman who wants her husband dead. He beats her and loses their kids in the park.

"Met her last week, friend of a friend, told her I'd take care of it."

Sal describes the target as an important guy at Goldman Sachs in Manhattan. Six foot three, 250 pounds, pasty faced, silver hair, Armani suits and ties. Prada Aviators, blue tint. No names.

"To answer the other questions: wherever you want, as soon as possible, however you want, 25K. Deal?"

She cocks her hand and slaps him on the cheek. Hard. "You're a cheap bastard."

"What the fuck?"

"Sal. I know the market is 50."

"Okay, 50, and to show you I'm not trying to take advantage, there's a hot new club over in the Meatpacking District, *Le Bain*, pool in the middle of the dance floor. Dinner at *Betony*. Meet you there at eight."

Before setting out, Sal had the hotel concierge arrange the evening, in case she looked as good as she sounded. And he was not disappointed.

"You're not too much of a bad fellow."

At eight-thirty, Sal's waiting at *Betony*; looking up at the gaudy gold ceiling panels, looking over the crowd huddled around the bar. He doesn't see, but hears her arrival: forks hit plates, bus boys drop trays of dishes. He looks up: Lana is sashaying across the floor toward him. A dress of pearlescent, diaphanous silk panels swishing side to side: promising to reveal, at the last moment, swinging back. He looks around. *Eat it guys, she's mine tonight.*

Dinner goes quickly (it seems that way), even after three hours: waiters hover, dishes are placed, emptied, removed, glasses filled and refilled. As they leave, she takes his arm and coos, "Very nice, Sal. Delicate forceful flavors. My compliments."

The door at *Le Bain* opens to thumping music. They're led to a private VIP lounge. Not Sal's doing. *Has she been here before? Did the concierge arrange it? The tip was generous.* Not complaining, only wondering. A bottle of Cristal is on the table, opened, poured in two glasses. Sal sits back, sips his champagne, Lana beside him, same relaxed posture, legs akimbo. She whispers, "Sal darling, I did a little research on our target after I left this afternoon. I don't think you told me everything."

"I knew we'd see one another again, so maybe I forgot some stuff."

"How silly of me, of course, that's it."

She clinks her glass against his. "And then there are the aspects that weren't quite accurate – bloody wrong in fact."

"Huh?"

"Pour us another glass. We should start with the description; no one in the New York office fits it."

"Details, details." Sal slurring his words now; thinks the champagne's getting to him. Not having the effect it usually does. Getting groggy, not sparkly.

She leans against him, her lips touching his ear. "Salvatore Giuseppe Mancuso, you are a foolish lad to think I would let you skim the fee. Fivefold difference, I think not."

Sal slumps over.

"I too have contacts on the West Coast." Lana presses a button beside the sofa. Two men appear.

"It appears my friend doesn't handle drink well. Your choice lads, East River or the Hudson."

In Our Lifetime

by Derek Osborne

Already the caterer and preset crews are busy. The wedding will be this Sunday. It is a beautiful late summer day, winds from the southwest at 10 -12, a deep blue sky and the island dull green and gray. Anja correctly read the writing on the wall last month when Andi had her meltdown. She's called in a bunch of favors from her 2nd Unit production subs. It pays to have good relationships in an industry full of snakes, not to mention the bragging rights for producing one of the hottest Hollywood weddings of the year in less than five weeks. People have flown in from everywhere. La senora is writing checks faster than the FED.

There is no such thing as an old, established Latin American family having a quiet, intimate affair. Combined with three more families on the Perkins' side the immediate guest list is topping one-fifty. Then there are all those friends who want to say goodbye but don't know how and Max thinks this might be a graceful way out. Throw in a few dozen show-biz folks and a few politico must-invites and, voila, it's up to three hundred. Add another fifty in servers, sous-chefs, bartenders, security, traffic control, sound and lighting, video, three helicopter pilots (it is an island) and don't forget the orchestra (twenty-three of Glenn Scott's best) – seat all the guests in five (count them) deluxe tents and the back lawn from the house to the water suddenly looks like Gatsby's in town. Even for Nantucket it's all pretty cool.

As expected, the paparazzi are out in force. If anyone is wondering where Rebecca gets her mischievous side they needn't look further. La senora has ordered a dozen Super Soakers, those monstrous water-pistols that jet out thirty feet, and pulled from her former life all the necessary skills in recruiting a young militia prepared to die for the cause. There are eleven nieces and nephews, ages ten to fifteen. For ammunition she has stockpiled five-gallon tins of grape juice. The children have permission to patrol the marsh and shoot on sight. For added measure, she has ordered a gallon of commercial-grade indigo fabric dye to enhance the juice. The troops have gone through rigorous training.

"I'm going out to the boat," Max announces after lunch. "I need some peace and quiet."

"I am coming with you."

"The hell you are."

"The hell I am not."

Rebecca has had on a walking cast for nearly a week. Her new name is *Ahab*.

"How will you get up the ladder?"

"Slowly."

Anja gives Eddie a look.

"I will take you both out," he says.

Down at the dinghy pier they notice two men unloading a Zodiac full of camera equipment. With Rorschach patterns of blue on their face, they look like they might have been shooting a remake of *Braveheart*. Rebecca starts laughing. She is dressed in a set of baggie sweats and a hoodie with glasses, and the men are so deep in their argument as to what went wrong and who is to blame they don't notice. Their money shot hobbles by unnoticed. Eddie pulls at the outboard and they are off. As a precaution, he speeds toward the west side of the anchorage and the Coast Guard Station; they'll double back behind the other boats.

The harbor is filled with cruising boats. It's the last week of the season. *Gadabout* needs more than a football field of room to swing on her mooring so she sits somewhat off from the others, out at the east end of the anchorage and in sight of the house. Nicky, one of the older nephews, has outfitted one of their dinghies into a kind of grape juice gunboat, complete with twin Super Soakers and several water balloon depth charges. The crew wear red bandanas and black t-shirts (la senora's idea); Anja made sure to alert the police and the Coast Guard. They patrol the perimeter of *Gadabout's* mooring, challenging all comers. Once in the cockpit, beneath the canopy, Rebecca and Max will have all the privacy and quiet they need. With the house so buzzed it's been hard to be alone. They both crave and fear this moment, impossible to know what will come; they have yet to have "the talk". For Max it will mean surrender; it will mean the cancer has won. For Rebecca, whenever she even gets near it, her entire being goes into a kind of stasis, a billion stabbing needles. She worries how it might be affecting the baby.

"Let's go down to the cabin," she says once they're on board.

"You want to revisit the scene of the crime?"

"I had not thought of that."

"If you fall again we'll never live it down."

She starts laughing. Just then a gust lifts the canopy. The same wind ripples the water's surface and swings the boat. *Gadabout* groans and sunlight pours into the cockpit. "We never did get to go sailing."

It's a test, a small regret compared to others. She waits to see how it affects their mood.

"Well, we can't have that. Especially on a day like today."

Max jumps up and heads down below. Rebecca sees the ICOM radio light up on the helm. He reappears and pulls the mic off the binnacle.

"Unit seven, unit seven this is unit nine, unit nine. Come back."

They have developed a code knowing the paparazzi will be monitoring the channels. A young girl's voice answers the hail.

"Unit nine this is seven switch channel C."

There are ninety-six channels to choose from. They have selected five and given them letters, choosing which to use at random. The children love this more than anything. They use Rebecca's favorite word – skullduggery. Max has to admit he's getting a kick out of it too.

"Christina?"

"Yes Uncle Max."

"I have a high priority mission for you, need to know, only."

"That means it's a secret, right?"

Christina is all of nine.

"Yes," Max says, looking at Rebecca, "it's a secret."

"Oh goodie."

"Tell Eddie and Anja we want to go sailing."

"Uncle Max, can I come?"

It's Nicky, Pam's oldest son. Pam, Maxes sister, has brought her entire brood, and, being farm kids, they have all been a great help. Max forgot they would all tune in.

"Yes, Uncle Max, can I come too?"

Now it is Pam, herself.

"Me too, Dad."

And Andi as well. Rebecca grabs the handset.

"Listen guys. Your Uncle Max and I came out to the boat to be alone. We realized I have never had the chance to go sailing on Gadabout. We wanted Eddie and Anja to come along as crew. Now that your Aunt Pam and Cousin Andi want to come I think that is also appropriate. How about we have a kid's sail tomorrow if the weather is nice? And Nicky, as head of security you must remain behind today so we can make the proper arrangements."

Max nods approval. Various disappointed mumbles of "okay" and "I guess" come over the handset.

"Can we come?"

It's a stranger's voice. Max is guessing their code wasn't too hard to crack. He takes the mic from Rebecca.

"Person requesting to tag along identify yourself."

"Just an interested party."

Whoever it is, judging from the accent, they're Italian. Another voice crackles on the handset.

"Interested Party, Interested Party this is US Coast Guard Nantucket Station, repeat, US Coast Guard Nantucket Station. Honor protocol and identify yourself."

For a moment the handset is dead.

"Ah, we are tourists visiting your lovely island."

The Coast Guard comes back. "Interested Party I repeat, identify your craft and position."

Rebecca is wearing that smile she gets whenever she knows she has won. Max is truly touched; they don't have to do this. The "Interested Party" has gone silent again. Nicky is pulling away and heading for the dinghy pier to pick up the others. The Coast Guard returns om the handset.

"Nantucket Harbor and all Interested Parties this is US Coast Guard. Be advised the yacht Gadabout is leaving the harbor. Be advised all unauthorized vessels approaching the yacht will be stopped and searched. We advise all Interested Parties to have their passports available. We advise all vessels have the proper number of floatation devices aboard, proper fuel management systems installed, engines inspected for the current year, craft registration documents in order. Any vessel in violation will be seized. Repeat, any vessel in violation will be seized. This is US Coast Guard, out."

"Gadabout, out."

Max is touched by what the Coast Guard is doing. He looks down at Rebecca. At first he thinks she is also appreciating their special treatment but sees something else is coming. She's trying to hold on but it's no use. He sits down beside her, places the flat of his hand on her belly. The tears begin, and when they do Max also loses control. So, he's thinking, the time has come. He grabs her and buries his face in her thick dark hair. There is no one else there to see them, no one else to comfort or worry about. And there is no one else to hear, so they allow this moment, the one they've been dreading, and there in the safety of *Gadabout's* cockpit come all the regrets, all the would haves and might have beens, all they now know will be certain. There is a strange, god-like wonder in it, what this child will mean not only for them but for everyone, what they must do to prepare.

"Thank you," Rebecca says after a time. She is laying on her side by now, her head nestled in Max's lap. Max can see the others approaching in one of the dinghies.

"My angel," he says. By the time Eddie and the others arrive they have dried their eyes and washed their faces. Max goes to the rail and greets each one in silence. He waves an acknowledgement to the kids in the grape-gun boat. He's hoping he'll have the strength to go with them tomorrow.

After the adults are on board he gives the command to raise all canvas. They will be sailing off the mooring, not a small feat and certainly not a maneuver for novices, but to seasoned sailors, aficionados, it is an act of both skill and purity. Eddie knows the drill. With Max at the helm, Andi and Anja man the winches. Pam tails the lines, coiling them in perfect order along the deck, a term all yachtsmen refer to as "Bristol". Rebecca sits silent. *Gadabout* glides past the other anchored yachts, their owners on deck, some with grand smiles and others looking like deer caught in the headlights. It's not every day a ninety foot ketch runs by your rail so close you could reach out and touch it. They're even flying the chute between the main and mizzen, a mass of billowing white, the bow of the boat cuts a clear path through the harbor. The Coast Guard's gunboat waits on station just outside the harbor's narrow entrance. Nicky and his fresh faced pirates follow astern. A lone photographer stands at the break-water, waiting for just the right moment when the boat and the lighthouse align with the blue and gray town behind, a once in a lifetime photo.

"Once in a lifetime," Max says to Rebecca.

"Our lifetime."

Gadabout heels. They are at sea.

Thursday

4

September
2014

Saving the Life
of the Dead

by Gloria Garfunkel

Every year I get into a Mixed Mood Episode, agitated and depressed leading up to the Jewish holidays. Rosh Hashanah and then 10 days of guilt-ridden repentance and then Yom Kippur, the final trial of whether you will live or die. Always irritable and act my worst this time of year. Eat lots of nonkosher food, especially bacon. Turn on the TV and drive a lot on the Sabbath. I'm daring God to kill me already. I drive extra fast. But that only leads to speeding tickets.

Chloe's mom and sister are here from Chicago and we're taking them out to lunch and dinner. I have to be on my best behavior which is torture because I'm in an irritable Mixed Mood Episode with a short fuse. We make small talk. I ask Chloe's sister about school. She's in ninth grade and in high school shock so she has plenty to say to fill in the conversation gaps. She's an adorable, skinny blonde, a smaller version of Chloe. Her mother is restrained and quiet. Preoccupied. Half in and out of the conversation.

Finally she says, "Chloe tells me you have bipolar. It's a terrible illness. You know it killed my husband. You know you two can never marry. The gene pools on both sides would make all your children bipolar. What a terrible legacy of doom to lay on them. You two should get out of this relationship now."

"You wish we hadn't been born, Mom?" asks Chloe.

Total silence for the rest of the meal. Chloe drives her mother and sister alone to the airport and doesn't say much when she returns.

"My mother still thinks she can save my father's life," is all she says. "She thinks it was her fault because they fought a lot."

Chartreuse

by John Wentworth Chapin

Eastern Antiques is a play on words: located on Eastern Avenue but filled with statuary and vases from Vietnam and Japan. Deonna, the owner, announces loudly to all new customers and window shoppers that the double entendre is fabulous, but she can't take full credit because it was Eastern Antiques before she bought it, back when it was filled with corroded brass fittings from ships dismantled in the Baltimore harbor a few blocks away. Now the shelves are lined with rows of identical porcelain laughing Chinese Buddhas, brass meditating Cambodian Buddhas, and decapitated stone Thai Buddhas.

"People *crave* them!" Deonna cackles. "How's that for irony?"

Charles sees a different irony; the stuff is certainly Eastern, but it's hardly antique. A few sumptuous Afghan carpets hanging from hooks in the back, beautiful but new, along with wooden tables made from medieval-looking temple doors salvaged from India – true artifacts but still newly made. The only actual antiques are locked in glass jewelry cases along a counter, and half that stuff looks faux-distressed. That's Deonna: antique and faux-distressed.

They unpack two wooden shipping crates. One more lies unopened; Charles and Deonna will be here late into the night, if the last couple of occasions are any indicator. She gets a new shipment every couple of weeks, and this is the third time Charles has helped her unload. He doesn't mind – she springs for Chinese food and they talk and he's getting paid and this is so much better than everything that has happened to him lately. When the customers are gone, she'll crack open a couple of bottles. Last time, they started with Grand Marnier and moved to a chablis, tonight it's Chartreuse. Mornings after are a wee bit rough, but they are entirely worth the feeling of being engaged in the world rather than worrying about how to be engaged with the world. Charles looks into his crystal ball and knows that this is exactly where he should be right now. Deonna is garish clothes. She is witty repartee. She is last-minute change of plans.

"This is a bigger shipment than usual," Charles says.

"I never know what I'm going to see until I unpack. Sometimes it takes three months, sometimes it's here on the next boat ... Every day is Christmas!" Deonna cackles, overly loud.

"Any idea what this is?" Charles says, pulling out a large round object swaddled in crinkly wrapping, more like magazine paper than packing paper. It's lightweight for its size.

"*Careful!*" Deonna shouts. "No bugs. This packing shit is full of bugs, so keep it in the crate."

No bugs, but there are flecks of dirt all over, as though someone packed raked leaves in there. Deonna explains that the thing he unwraps is a yaksha head – a guardian spirit. It has exaggeratedly vicious features and vibrant colors, more demon than spirit to Charles.

Deonna says, "Let me know if you see a – oh, YAY!" She suddenly throws raffia everywhere from her crate. She lifts a stack of day-glo green cloths, tied in a bundle. "They're here! I LOVE these! Look at them! OH!"

She holds it out for Charles's inspection. The fabric shimmers and melts in her hands like mercury.

"What is it?" Charles asks.

35

"They are – really, you don't know? Well, hold on a second!" Deonna bends over to suck down the last of her apéritif, gives Charles a sloppy excited pat on the hand, and then dashes to the storeroom clutching the silks.

Charles continues with the half-dozen yaksha heads in the crate that need unwrapping. One is heavier than the rest, and Charles feels something moving inside. He flips it over and finds there a plastic container stuffed into the hollow cavity. He pulls it out; inside rests an acid green velvet pouch, the sort of little bag you'd expect to package cufflinks or expensive liqueur.

Charles shakes from the bag, gently onto the glass counter, two things: a tiny plastic zipper storage bag with a tablespoon of cut, colored gemstones and a dark, brown-green brick the size of a deck of playing cards, wrapped in saran wrap and a healthy dose of tape.

Gems and something that is probably not chocolate.

He looks up. Deonna stands in the doorway, shoulders bare, wearing a thin piece of fabric wrapped around her midsection, the silk acting as a halter top and pressing desiccated old breasts against her bony chest. She stares at Charles and the bag and its contents.

It's weird. He's gotten plenty of weirdness from her over the last few weeks, but this is something new. He imagines her pulling out a revolver and wasting him on the spot. But where would she keep it? She's practically naked, which is making this all the weirder.

She saunters over to him, the tops of her breasts firmly tourniqueted in place and the bottoms swinging freely against the thin fabric. "If you think you're going to grab my stash, you've got another thing coming."

Charles begins to stutter a response.

Deonna picks up the brown-green brick. "But if you want to help me make brownies, we're golden."

"It's – what is it?"

"You've never seen hash before?"

Charles shakes his head.

Deonna says, "I don't approve of the look on your face, Judge Judy. It's for my personal consumption."

When Charles thinks of all the things that he cares too much about, the things that upset him, the things that set him off – well, this certainly is not one of them. He says, quietly, "No. I don't care."

"Well I think you do care, from what I can see," she says. "Your body language is all tense and you're getting defensive. I get high sometimes. That's the deal."

"It's more that I didn't expect to find a velvet bag of contraband inside a demon's head."

"Yaksha. They're benevolent guardian spirits. It's kind of a joke that – my contact put it in there."

Hilarious, Charles thinks. *Nothing funnier than a droll smuggler.* "What's up with the gemstones?"

"I can get a lot more for them here than he can over there. I grease his palm with cash and he greases mine with hash. Ha! That's a poem!" she crows as she grabs the Chartreuse and pours them both another shot.

Charles waves goodnight to Deonna and fumbles with his car keys. He's never smoked hash before, but he feels more numb than mellow. Maybe it's the Chartreuse. Maybe it's what Deonna said before he left. Charles pulls out into the street, and then stops before he knows why he's stopping. The flashing lights of a police cruiser race down the block toward him. It zooms past, siren wailing into the distance. His chest thumps.

He thinks back to Deonna slurring, tottering against an empty crate. "You were in rehab. You've got a record, bub. You were mixed up in a whole lotta nasty. Last thing you need is the Baltimore Police department snooping around your garbage cans, if you get my drift. You can keep your mouth shut, right?"

Charles nodded when she said this. He attributed it to ugly drunkenness; Charles had discovered a possibly damaging fact about her, and she was doing some risk management.

But now, thumping chest rattling his ribs, pounding in his ears, he remembers how they met: he announced that he had just left rehab, and then he wailed about the string of death and misfortune that trailed him. She offered him the job because she's a drunk and thinks he's one too – but now he sees a broader view. She believes she has found herself a patsy.

He doesn't want her gemstones or her greasy drugs, but she's too blind to see this. Charles may not know what he wants, but he knows what he doesn't want.

To be used. To be yet another woman's patsy.

He hopes he's sober enough to remember this in the morning. He puts the car back into gear and heads home.

Saturday

6

September
2014

Tick

by Lynn Beighley

My cat, Pollock, is an indoor cat. He'd prefer not to be, but I'd prefer him to not become a gray cat pancake on the busy street in front of my apartment.

His current favorite perch is on the back of my couch. It looks out on a tiny balcony I never use. Last spring, a pair of confused robins mistook the railing for a tree limb. They produced one perfect egg. Once in a while, I'd sit next to Pollock as he waited for mom and dad robin to stop by. Me, I'd stare at the blue egg. Instead of trying to decide what the TV watching public wanted me to do, or what Bill Plover would do next, or if I was out of wine, I'd look at the egg. My eyes would lose focus (more often when I wasn't out of wine) and the egg would go from being a small blue sphere and become an entire (often fuzzy) universe.

And then it hatched. I don't know exactly when. I've been distracted. I went out with my dad on Thursday to help him drink his sorrows away. His fiancée left him. She wasn't willing to fly to Vegas for a quick, cheap wedding after I refused to let the *You Tell Me* reality show people foot the bill in exchange for my and Bill Plover's attendance. I'm still seething that he asked me, and he still doesn't entirely understand why I didn't want to do it. But he didn't mind me buying him many drinks, and by the end of the evening, Dad was ready to admit that she was in it for the fame. He probably doesn't remember that concession, but it's there, in his addled brain.

And Seamus spent last night here. Very distracting.

After he left this morning, I carried my bowl of cereal to peer out with a riveted Pollock, and my egg was gone, and in its place ...

Remember *Return of the Jedi*? This one scene? Our heroes, Leia in a gratuitous bikini, are with Jabba the Hut on this hovering spaceship platform thing, hanging out over the desert. Beneath them is the gaping maw of some kind of horrible creature that will take a very long time to digest them. I remember it's supposed to take a thousand years. Yeah, okay, whatever.

Anyway, that blue egg I adored has been replaced by the gaping maw beast. Granted, on a smaller scale, but horrific all the same. (The nasty creature is called a Sarlacc, in case you were wondering. And the good guys do avoid getting digested by it, surprise.)

I can't figure out how such an enormous mouth could have come out of that egg. I watch in disgusted fascination as mom and dad take turns stuffing worms and bugs into it. It never closes. Pollock waits for the parents, I can't look away from the chick monster's pie hole. Without looking, I reach over to scratch Pollock under his chin. I'm pretty good at this, and he helps. My fingers touch his jaw and brush across a small, hard bump that isn't supposed to be there.

I look and see that Pollock, my indoor cat, has a tick. I hate ticks. I am proud that I do not scream or squeal. I do run to the bathroom and scrub my hand.

How did he get a tick? Did it come in on me? Or Seamus? I'm not sure how I'm supposed to get it off him. I remember something about Vaseline, something about a lit match you blow out, something about the tick head not being a good thing to leave in the creature. I dig around for tweezers, a pair I don't like, but I can only find my favorite ones.

Armed with my best tweezers, a jar of Vaseline, a book of matches, a towel, a box of tissues, a couple Band-Aids, and an old ashtray, I approach Pollock. He knows I'm up to something and leaps off the couch and dashes into my room, to hide, no doubt, in my closet.

I wander into the kitchen to run the can opener and lure him out. I run the can opener and my phone rings. I answer it, hoping it's Seamus, hoping I can get him to come over and take over the tick removal for me.

And it is Seamus.

"Hey sweetie," he says, "listen, there's a guy from the show here and he has an idea for us to make a lot of money, and I know how you feel about all this stuff, but Jenn, honey, please hear me out."

Pollock stands at the entrance of the kitchen, looking at me. Without speaking, I quietly hang up the phone.

Sunday

7

September
2014

Moirologia

by Andrew Stancek

You are every child who believes in the "happily ever after." You are ordinary and everything that happened to you is extraordinary. You show that dreams come true, that the impossible is possible, that sense is not necessary.

You are Clark Kent and Peter Pan and an ordinary kid, sick and with a strange name, living in an ordinary home.

You speak with a squeaky voice and a stutter and you sweat under the hot TV lights and you cannot explain and you are more lovable and more believable.

You walk funny. Maybe it's the sickness with the wacky name or maybe the months in bed. You don't quite limp but when we replay the footage we see that every now and then your legs don't align and your walk is off-kilter and you are every funny-looking funny-walking kid.

You don't shill for money on TV, don't go on tour, don't sell subscriptions to your site. You don't have a site. You are free. Every inventor in the history of the world, every guru, every speaker has passed the hat to the admiring crowds but you don't.

Every one of them wants to convert you to their image, to harness you to their needs but you remain you.

Then we realize that you not only won't merge for them, you won't merge for us either. You turn away from us, too.

You leave us behind.

When it dawns on us that we will not become you, we start to hate you.

You cannot be known.

You cannot be understood.

You cannot be saved.

Monday

8

September
2014

Really Weird Shit

by Rachel Ambrose

Frederico's into some really weird shit.

I've figured this out over the past three weeks. And maybe my definition of "really weird shit" is getting skewed, because the other day I looked at a painting of a baby angel making love to a girl baby demon and thought, "wow, how adorable," instead of, "someone should send that painter to a shrink."

"Yeah, and he's really mysterious, like he'll leave these giant gaps in his calendar and when I go to fill them in, he's like, just leave them open," I'm telling Isa as I get ready for the monthly open gallery show in September. "Like entire afternoons."

"Is he ... I don't know, a serial stalker? A secret nudist?" Isa asks, munching on tortilla chips out of the bag as she stands in the bathroom doorway. "Maybe he has some super rare medical condition that makes it impossible for him to work for more than four hours a day."

"I dunno," I say, putting down my mascara and grabbing my lipstick. "Probably some standing sex appointment with his wife. When else would he have time? He makes me feel really smart, though, which is a new thing for me. Blake was always so condescending, like, yes baby-waby you got the answer right, good girl, want a biscuit?" I shake my head. "I can't believe I thought he was good for me."

"That's twice today," Isa remarks, and I frown at her from the mirror. "Twice today you mentioned Blake. That's down from three times yesterday, so that's progress!" She does a little victory dance and I smile. Getting this job and leaving Mrs. Hatfield were really the best decisions I've made in a long time. Keeping track of Frederico is an easy job for me, given my slightly obsessive nature. Right at this moment, I can tell Isa that he's probably finishing dinner with his family and aims to be at the gallery in half an hour to start on setting up for the show.

"Is it creepy that I always know where he is?" I ask.

"A little," concedes Isa, nodding. "But think of how good that makes you, as his assistant! I bet he never lets you go."

"We can only hope," I say, giving myself one last look in the mirror. "Okay, I think I'm ready to do this, I'll see you later!" I grab my purse and head out the door, making sure to remember the crackers and cheese I've promised to bring. One more good thing about this job is that it's made me far less absent-minded than I used to be. The first week I went around completely neurotic and sure I'd forget something, but when I did (I double-booked Frederico in two meetings at once by mistake), the world didn't end! He just frowned at me and told me, "Don't do it again." So I haven't ... yet. It's amazing what you can accomplish when quiet excellence is expected of you. And I'm well paid for it, to boot!

I sweep into the gallery twenty minutes later, a bottle of white wine in my handbag, and start assembling the snacks. Frederico likes what he calls "little bits" – in food as well as in art. He'll pick up an origami swan that someone threw in the trash and turn it into the inspiration for Oscar De La Renta's next summer gown. I fan out the paper napkins and straighten the blue cheese as I wave to Edie, my coworker. She's a junior curator at the museum, and Frederico is her boss too. "Oh, have you seen the new watercolor that

Blake Easton put together?" she says, leaning down to mutter in my ear. I turn, startled. Damn Blake. Can't he just get out of my life for one night? "It's *awful*," she says gleefully, and I laugh in relief. Of course it is.

Cold Comfort

by Gill Hoffs

My sinuses feel as tight as a virgin's twat, I stink of menthol, and I have sex-doll lips parted in a chapped 'O' because I'm so bunged up I have to mouth-breathe.

But today's client is only in town for one night. And the only girl he wants for his dinner at Parasols 'n' Parsnips is mucoussy me. Delightful.

I feel like today *I'm* the one renting my body, and it isn't a comfortable fit.

I spend the day in a steam room near his hotel, dumping herbal waters on the coals until my eyes smart and stream and my chest aches and nipples tingle. Come five o'clock, I'm as clear of snot as possible and a cold shower beckons. I rinse the stink away, and can't help noticing the other women's glances at my crotch. This client's Canadian and it's autumn so my pubes are currently cropped into a maple leaf, dyed red, a treat for him tonight. Let them look. It's fabulous.

A quick dash to the office, where Zoe has my outfit and a mug of Lemsip ready and waiting, and I'm ready to go. My co-ordination's off and the heels don't help so I bang into the doorframes and ricochet down the corridor like I'm in a pinball machine on the way to the car. The driver opens the door for me, probably hoping for a squint up my skirt, and I bend over from the waist allowing the fabric to reveal my lack of underwear because why the hell not but then my usual poise deserts me and I clunk my head on the way in, and what started as sexy becomes stupid instead.

"Are you alright, love? I felt that meself."

I rub the side of my head carefully, trying not to muss my hair, and sniff back the snot that so annoyingly insists on accompanying anything that makes my eyes water. Like an Audi to the head, for example.

"I'm fine, I'm fine."

I don't mean to snap at him but I'm really not fine, and clouting my skull on the car didn't help. We settle into our seats, strapping ourselves in and pointedly not meeting each other's eyes in the mirror, then drive through the drizzle to his hotel. A doorman with hazel eyes and a scurfy moustache opens the car door and this time I manage not to make contact with anything I shouldn't on my way out. He touches his index finger to the brim of his fancy hat as I walk past him with a smile and the tiniest of handbags toward the elevator. The woman on the front desk gives me the side-eye as I sniff my way past, so I deliberately slow my walk and keep my movements calm and dignified so as to dispel any notion she has of me as a cokehead.

I make it to the lift unchallenged, step in, press button 21, and sneeze.

Fuck-a-doodle-do.

I have enough floors between me and my 'date' to blow my nose long and loud, wipe my upper lip, check my lipstick and bogie status in my mirror, and tuck the damp tissue back into my bag beside my Olbas oil, lozenges, and sachets of strawberry lube. Zoe's already arranged with room service to hide a bottle of maple syrup in the bedside cabinet, so we're all set for the pre-dinner activities. I hope.

§

We start off well. I sit on the desk where only this afternoon he signed some multi-national deal, spread my legs and hold my skirt high.

"A maple leaf, eh? I love it! Good girl!"

He stuffs a finger in and I smile and squirm and wish he'd had a manicure. Hangnails can *hurt*.

He scoops me up, both hands on my arse, and throws me on the bed with an "Oof", which makes me revise my estimate of his age (60s? maybe?) instead of how happy I am with my weight.

I wriggle out of my dress and throw it near the door as he unzips his easy-iron trousers – they're expensive and suited to a busy day of travel and deals but still, easy-iron, ugh – and frees his cock from stripy blue briefs. I hold up a finger and murmur "Wait ..." as I retrieve the bottle of syrup from the tiny cupboard where it lurks beside the Gideon bible, then hold it up where he can see it.

He actually claps, thrilled at the fun of it, I think – his notes said he was *very* patriotic – and watches while I pour a little on my crotch and breasts then dribble more from a height onto my outstretched tongue. I put the bottle back near the bible then he pounces and all I feel are whiskers, tongue, and teeth.

I'm alternately too hot and too cold. Fever is definitely upon me. I can retreat to my own bed in my own flat with a wheatbag and my cat and my softest comfiest pyjamas in just under seven hours. I'm desperate for a cup of hot sweet tea and a sleep. But there's maybe half a dozen 'orgasms' to get through first.

My being poorly is proving a turn-on for my client, though. When I shiver and tremble he interprets it as need. When my skin prickles and goosebumps, he sees only erect nipples and chews them like winegums. When I mouth-breathe, he thinks I'm getting off on his sticky fumbling.

Then he digs his hands under my back and hefts me on top of him as he rolls onto his. When he snogs me I taste myself and too much maple syrup on his teeth, and I can't mouth breathe which is a disaster for my nostrils. I shudder with another flash of feeling frozen to the core and disengage from his face before he notices the snot coursing down my upper lip. It's much easier to hide your face with a blowjob.

I suck and lick and try not to sniff too loudly.

"Bend over. I *need* to fuck that wee pussy, *right* now, eh?"

Shit, my head's not with it, the lube's out of reach in my bag over by the desk. Instead of wiping my nose on the bedding I pinch a slick of it from my nostrils and dab it on the head of his cock, drip some spit on it, and crawl off him on all fours. My joints are aching and my crotch doesn't want any visitors today, thank you. Every cell of my vagina is shouting "Closed for business!" but I've got a job to do and he's a repeat client, and a good one, so there's no way I'm bowing out.

He takes me from behind and I fall over.

Somehow I manage to keep my arse in the air and not look like a total idiot, splayed on the bed. He finishes off with a spurt and a squirt and a "Whooooo!" and slaps my bottom as I roll over and collapse next to him.

"Clean me up, gorgeous – we've got time to go again before dinner."

I smile, of course, and clamber over to his cock. I lick and slurp and sniff – the latter as quietly as possible – and feel the first prickling of a sneeze building in my nose. Fuck.

I try to switch to just hands for a moment until my nose clears and the crisis passes but as I draw my head away his hands push me back onto his cock and keep me there. I would redirect the head of it into my cheek, safely away from my teeth, but he's giving me no room to manoeuvre. I put all my energy into sucking him off, hoping – no doubt in vain – that he'll miraculously spunk in the next few seconds before my nose goes nuclear.

What other info did he have on his form? What can I do to speed him up? My head's so foggy I doubt I'd remember my mobile number at this point. Finger in the arse? Worth a shot. I squirm my pinky in past some crusty stuff I try not to think about, glad I can't smell a thing, and he groans and pants and clamps my head down harder.

On the plus side, he's clearly building up to blow.

The negative, however, is that his pubes are now tickling inside my nostrils.

I can't help it.

With his dick in my mouth and my nose full of snot, I sneeze.

The only plus side to this is that my teeth don't quite meet.

Saying "Gesundheit" really isn't enough.

Wednesday

10

September
2014

Peter Pan Collar

by Susan Tepper

Fall was when they used to outfit him for school in freakish short pants and checkered suspenders and a white button shirt with a round collar. High socks and brown leather tie shoes. The other boys called him *Peter Pan collar* and smeared dirt and their own snot on his face. He cried every morning begging to stay home. Out came the belt. He ran out the back door with the neighbor's geese hot on his trail. Those geese came in a flock. Before he could head the other way, five or more blocking the road to the school bus. Beaks open. Squawking and snapping at his bare legs.

Taking the beer opener kept on the floor next to the brake pedal, using the sharp edge, he pares his fingernails. Car windows rolled down. It's a good day. Warm but not too warm. Over the summer he let his nails grow till they curled too: yellow and dirty. It felt right. He settles his weight in the car's bucket seat. Clock on the dash shows 11:03. In no time they'll be out for recess. The first bunch of little darlings. They'll run and shout and squeak and squeal. Fly if they could. Spread their arms and fly like Peter Pan. That's what gave him the idea to take a new name. Fresh. Start over. Fuck Kavanagh and all the fucking Kavanagh family. P. Pedersen. That is it.

If he can just nab one small boy his day will be complete. Tuck the kid in the trunk, set up all soft and blankety for ease of transport. Drive a few towns over, up the hill behind the reservoir. Back where the pines make thick walls. Open the trunk, take him out and love him. Love him to pieces.

Pedersen feels a woody coming on. He smiles. Pets it. Same as he pets the white rat Swoon.

The Cross to Bear

by Jessica McHugh

News of his mother's stroke pushes Father Edward McKenzie toward Shady Grace Retirement Home faster than he'd expected. The head nurse greets him at the door, her rotund physique testing the limits of her faded violet scrubs. Roberta's wardrobe outside of the retirement home isn't much better. While her floral church dresses flirt with a wider color scheme, the bulky shapes are just as unflattering, squeezing and segmenting her flesh in all the wrong places. Edward often wishes he could bring out her natural beauty with a makeover.

Really, Edward, I don't think this an appropriate time to ponder this.

Grandma Eleanor is right, as usual, but her voice makes him realize it's the first time she's spoken since he received the call from Shady Grace. Betty is her daughter. In spite of the difficulties they shared while Eleanor was alive, he assumed she would have some sort of reaction to her daughter's stroke. Even if it were only the fear that Betty would soon join her in the afterlife.

Though she's adopted a more somber tone than usual, Nurse Roberta's sunshine can't be hidden behind the dark clouds of the day. As they plod to his mother's room, Edward wrings his crucifix throughout her explanation of Betty McKenzie's condition.

"Your mother suffered a Transient Ischemic Attack, also know as a 'baby stroke'," she says. "I know the nickname doesn't make it any cuter, but these attacks are thankfully mild. Ms. McKenzie is asleep now, but we expect her to make a full recovery. She's a tough old bird."

"Yes, I know," Edward says.

Betty was tough when she ridiculed him as a child, tough when she tried to "cane the fairy out of him" as a teenager, and even tougher after he took the cloth. She never thought it was appropriate for him to conceal his true desires behind God and the church, and he agrees now. But not so cruelly. Edward doesn't think it's wrong to hide a corset beneath his vestments; he's just tired of hiding.

Roberta opens the door into Betty's room, and the first thing Edward sees is the cardiac monitor, its screen marked with colorful squiggles and digits. His mother lies beneath a crisp white sheet, her skin more jaundiced than ever. The nasal cannula delivering her oxygen whistles. Roberta shuffles over to inspect it, but Edward stops her.

"I don't want to wake her yet."

Roberta nods as she pats his shoulder. "I understand. Take your time, Father."

She closes the door when she leaves. Only then does Edward notice the drippy stain on the back, like someone had hurled a liquor bottle at the door. Staring at his sallow mother in the hospital bed, he figures it's an all-too-accurate assumption.

Edward has seen folks in far worse circumstances at Shady Grace. More machines. Less consistent breathing. As a priest, he's compelled to sit beside Betty's bed like he does in those dire situations, to hold her hand, to ease her heart and mind by assuring her that she has a place in God's Heaven. But as her oft-abused son, he refuses to take one step in her direction.

Instead, he leans against her dresser, his gaze captured by the glimmer of glass in the top drawer. He grits his teeth as he removes and drops the empty vodka bottle in the trash. He pockets the other he finds, still sloshing with liquor. Some of the vodka has spilled in the drawer, staining many of the old photographs inside. Several are ruined, the alcohol distorting Betty's youthful face, but after pushing them aside, he finds unsullied pictures of his mother as a young girl, the unmistakable glint of hope filling her eyes.

May I?

He hands one of the pictures to Eleanor, who sighs.

"She was so full of life," Edward says, "So hopeful."

She was posing. After this picture was taken, she went right back to being who she was.

Eleanor digs deeper into the drawer and finds a photo of Edward as a child. Gazing at it, her face warms.

Now, this is someone who never poses, never pretends.

Edward snatches the photo from her, his jaw clenched. He can't remember the day the photo was taken, or how Betty had gotten him to smile – until he squints at the photo. Seeing his mother's ballet flats on his tiny feet, he sighs in remembrance. As a child, he would often slip them on while she was away, delighting in the crisp scrape of the leather against their splintered kitchen floor, and how the force of his clumsy pirouettes would occasionally toss them across the room.

He'd been unable to ditch them before Betty arrived home the day the photo was taken. She'd snapped it, ignorant of the shoes until he'd started shuffling away. Tearing them off his feet, she threw the ballet flats out the window, declaring them "tainted" before caning Edward's bottom bloody.

Dropping the picture back in the drawer, Edward whispers. "I never pretend? That's all I do, Grandmother. I've been posing for a picture all my life."

Not at the Paradiso Club.

"And we saw how well that turned out."

Staring at the sticky snapshots of a life misled, Edward can't muster one memory in which Betty appears as happy as in the pictures. Worse, he can say the same about himself.

He shuts the drawer with a sigh. Eleanor touches his shoulder, but it's not as comforting as it once was.

You aren't alone, Edward. You understand that, right?

Facing his grandmother, he nods. "I do. All too well."

Betty McKenzie snorts. Seeing her struggling to sit up, Edward dashes to her side, but she waves him away.

"How are you feeling?" he asks.

She narrows her eyes and croaks. "Oh, Edward, I feel so many things. About my failures, mostly." He sits beside her, pleased that the stroke has made her introspective until she adds, "I wish I'd never had a child. You, especially."

He lowers his head, twisting his crucifix as he says, "We can't choose who our children will grow up to be, any more than those children can choose their mothers. Or change them."

Edward tries to stop her as she wrestles with the nasal cannula, but she hisses, pulls it from her nostrils and hurls it at him.

"You shouldn't have come," she says. "This is all your fault."

"I think the empty bottle of booze in the trashcan is more at fault than I am."

She wheezes. "Maybe so, but I was drinking because of the rumor I heard about you. That you tarted yourself up, went out in public as a woman, and fucked some stranger."

Edward's innards tremble and twist. "Where did you hear that?"

"Geraldine Kitner. She said her son stopped into some homo bar for directions and saw you dressed as a woman, throwing your disgusting lifestyle in everyone's face."

As she shakily draws her yellowed face closer to Edward, her skin appears to sag even more. But beneath the wizened flesh, her attitude is hard and clenched. "Go on," she says. "Tell me it's not true."

Imagining the oversized ballet flats on his feet, Father Edward McKenzie smiles. His toes grip the soles of his shoes like he used to with the slippers, holding them to feet through illusory spins and high kicks.

"No," he says. "I didn't sleep with anyone, but I won't deny the rest."

Betty's stomach lurches, and she covers her mouth as she swallows hard.

"I'd say 'I have no son,' but that would probably make you happy, wouldn't it?" Wrapping her claw around his crucifix, she tears it from his neck. "This is a family heirloom. Since I have no child, it belongs with me."

"It's Grandma Eleanor's, and she wants me to have it."

"Eleanor is dead. She doesn't want anything anymore," Betty says. "Even when she did, I wasn't in the habit of giving her what she wanted."

Edward stands, his hand resting on his chest. Turning away from Betty, he says, "I'll tell Roberta you're awake. I'm certain she'll be disappointed."

He opens the door to leave, but the sound of two women asking the same question stops him. Together, Eleanor and Betty say, "You're not going to try to take it back?"

Standing beside her daughter's bed, Eleanor's face drains of its color. Her face creases in confusion, and her hands shake as she reaches out. Eleanor has always been infinitely kinder and more beautiful than Betty, but for the first time, Edward recognizes how closely they resemble one another.

"No," he replies, smiling at the crucifix. "I don't need it anymore."

The Displeasure Principle

by Shane Simmons

"Sorry it's been a while since we last got together. Girlfriend's been dealing with a family crisis and she really needed me." He looks rougher than usual and rubs his tired eyes.

In my presence, Callum says very little about his live-in girlfriend. But when he does there comes across an affection. On one hand, how can someone be quite willing to sneak around behind their loved one's back, and yet still seem to be entirely in love with that person? I've come to the conclusion that what they *have* and what we *do* are entirely separate beasts. And I suppose for him they can co-exist quite peacefully without rattling each other's cage.

For me, I've begun to crave something more.

"What was the crisis?"

"Her dad's been diagnosed with Parkinson's. He's only in his early forties." He twiddles his thumbs amongst the forest of hair covering his torso. "She's been pretty cut up about it."

A revolting pang of jealousy appears from out of nowhere. I push it down as hard as I can but I find myself remembering back, stood alone in the living room of the old house, two police officers before me. Telling me my parents had been involved in a crash. Their car had careered off the side of a bridge onto the road below. They told me the paramedics had tried their best to save them.

Their words blurred mid-air, passed right through me, slo-mo. Nothing registering. Slipping into shock, I'd begun to tremble.

I remember wanting no one other than Mark in that room with me.

I'd never felt so alone.

I give him a peck on his cheek. "She's lucky to have you."

He rolls over, already spent and I'm lying next to him, finishing myself off. I'm staring up at the ceiling, trying to think of something, anything to make this work. But I tug, pull, stroke, and nothing. If only he'd give me a hand (or even better, a mouth) but he lost interest seconds after he came.

I give up, my hands slide down limp at my side. I can hear his breathing next to me, in and out. His 'phone chirps from somewhere on the floor.

His eyes snap open, "Fuck," he says, jumping out of the bed, "sorry, you can't stay tonight."

"Girlfriend coming home?"

He's clambering to pull on his jeans. I'm reaching to pull on mine.

In the hall I pick up the rucksack I'd packed this morning with my toothbrush, some deodorant and fresh clothes for tomorrow. I turn to find he's already opened the door.

"I'll text you sometime soon."

As I retrace my route to the train station, in the back of my mind there's a niggling. I know what the deal is.

On the opposite platform is a heaving mass of bodies, tarted up, heading out for a night uptown. It's only just gone seven and the night is early, but when all working days begin blurring into one and you have no real plans, the arrival of the weekend is a non-event.

Going along with Sandra and her idea of 'fun' was maybe where this all went wrong. For her, simply having a lie-in lay is all the 'fun' she needs. She kids herself that it means something more, and yet she still never fails to seem far happier than myself.

And Callum somehow manages to have his cake and eat it. I suppose that makes me a bit jealous.

I step onto a train that will soon be heading in the opposite direction to the razzmatazz uptown. The carriage is crammed with city suits and briefcases, all heading home after work.

You see those people, the ones who get married and end up having affairs? And when they (inevitably) get caught, they always come out with that line, "But they meant nothing." It never soothes the wounds, but perhaps there's an element of truth. Maybe that 'other' person never really meant a thing beyond fleeting moments. And I no longer want to be that 'moment'.

Sandra thinks I need someone, anyone, and I don't think I do.

The only reason I bothered responding to Callum's texts and going out of my way to get up to his place was the nights spent playing Xbox games like a pair of teenagers, sharing a post-session takeaway and talking aimlessly about anything and everything.

I don't *need* Callum's body. And I don't *need* Mark, who's just a dying memory, slowly going out of view on the horizon. I don't *need* anyone. Not just yet.

Next month I turn twenty-three. Sandra had already talked about going out for my birthday do. In her mind she'd already invited herself, Marlon and Callum in tow.

Funny that, when it isn't herself being cheated on her morals on such matters really don't count for much ... I don't *do* birthdays. I'd like to run away for the week. Do what I want to do, go where I want to go. A few seats free up on the train. I sit down and take out my 'phone, type 'city breaks' into Google.

Where could I go?

Looking down at my 'phone I find my eyes distracted by a shape under the taut grey sateen trousers of the suit opposite. I shake my head and get back to more pressing matters. Where could I go?

A text message interrupts my browsing.

"Sorry bout tonite. Msg ya 4 a hook up soon."

"I think it's for the best that we leave it there mate," I type into my 'phone. "Best of luck to you."

I'm smiling as I close the messages and return to looking over pretty photos of cities, cobbled streets by night, sunlit scenes, winding canals.

"Shit!" I jump up as I see the sign for my station sliding away from the train. Too late, no point in pushing through the people blocking the aisle, so I sit back down and wait.

Getting off at the next stop, I walk over the bridge to the opposite platform. Once again my 'phone calls for attention. It's Callum.

"????"

After hitting delete I go into my contacts and erase his number too. It's empowering, doing just what you feel. When I get in I'm going to order myself a Chinese. Put the 'phone on silent. Book myself a birthday break away.

"Yes, why the fuck not," I think to myself, as I step onto another train.

Sand

by Michelle Elvy

They arrive at the beach and Ellie parks the car. Stevie pays the meter – two hours. Manny unfolds from the back seat and stretches. Sylvie is already racing to the water, her small feet kicking up sand with each happy stride. A day at the beach. One last trip before Stevie heads south.

They've driven across the low flatlands of the eastern shore to get here – across the Bay Bridge and east, cornfields blurring, acre after acre. A trip Stevie has made a hundred times. He's feeling nostalgic today – Ellie at the wheel, Manny and Sylvie in the back, playing Go Fish on the seat between them. He and Manny played Go Fish when they were kids. Go Fish and Minecraft, Tomb Raider and Poker. They started stealing cars when they got bored with all the rest, but that only lasted a year or so. In January they veered way off course, all of them. They've been crawling their way back to the center ever since. Stevie has wondered all year whether that flight through the sky, when he was hurled from the car while the others tumbled and rolled together – Lucky going through the windshield and ending everything they knew up until then – put him on this outward-reeling trajectory and marked the beginning of his long goodbye. He can't fight centrifugal force. He has tried to come back to the center – graduating and getting into college, helping Manny graduate too. Even his relationship with Ellie is an effort to hold fast.

And yet he's leaving. Manny's running his dad's garage, Ellie's got an internship with the Chesapeake Bay Foundation – reasons to stay. But Stevie's deferred college for a year and in some ways is already gone.

Manny jogs down to the beach after Sylvie but Ellie comes around to Stevie's side of the car and leans into him. They kiss. She smells like summer, even now. Salt. Sugar. Sun. He will never forget this smell. He nods to the package lying on the front seat. "What is it?" He wants to open it and see the treasure Ellie has placed inside, but he also wants to keep it exactly as it is, neatly wrapped in its square box.

"It's for you. Something from here." He thinks she means here, as in *this place*, the geography they have all been born into, but as she says it Ellie's hand goes to her locket around her neck and rests near her heart. Stevie looks from the package on the seat to Ellie and thinks *What the hell, maybe I won't leave after all, maybe I'll stay here, maybe I'll get snowed in if I stay long enough, maybe I'll spend the winter plowing driveways or skating on a frozen lake or just holding Ellie's hand.*

His stomach churns at that small gesture. Hand on heart. Up to this moment, he's been pretty sure he's leaving forever.

"I'm not leaving forever, you know."

"You never know. Besides, you haven't read this."

Stevie unwraps the paper and opens the box. Inside is a book. A hard cover. He turns it over in his hands. "Ellie, this isn't just any book."

"I know."

"You can't give me this."

"Yes I can." She touches his shoulder, leans in, her forehead against his. She is exactly the same height and

64

their foreheads and noses and then lips touch again. Her wind-blown hair tickles his cheek; her hand cups the back of his neck. Her breath is pulling him in, stilling the restlessness inside.

She inhales, pulls back. Stevie looks at the book in his hands. A first edition of William Warner's *Beautiful Swimmers*, with an inscription: *To Tom, one of the finest few*. Signed by the author.

One of the few things Ellie has from her grandfather, Tom. There are untold stories about Tom and his son, Ellie's dad, both part of a long line of fishermen. Ellie has always been connected to the Chesapeake in a way that Stevie only remotely gets. He feels the vague notion that this is where he's from, sure – with parents from DC and his own life playing out in its entirety in this low flatland of sorghum and corn, lacrosse and summer lightning storms. But for Ellie, this is where she *belongs*. Her grandfather Tom was a waterman on one of the last skipjacks of the Chesapeake. He dredged for oysters on his traditional boat, the *Maryanne of the Choptank*, all through the 1960s and 70s and even into the 80s. He gave countless hours to William Warner in a long series of conversations that eventually turned into the Pulitzer-winning book. He dropped dead of a heart attack the year Ellie was born.

Stevie knows Ellie is attached to her mostly missing family members more than those alive – her grandfather and father, also lost unexpectedly to the hard work of the mostly benign waters of the Chesapeake, and her uncle, a man who moved inland to raise cattle in an effort to escape his waterborne birth right and all the expectations associated with it, who was then crushed in a freak tractor accident. For as long as Stevie has known Ellie, her only remaining family, besides Sylvie, has been her mother, who is scarcely there, preferring vodka to raising two daughters and usually holed up with her weird cousin in a far corner of Pennsylvania. There have been glimpses of Grace, but they are never happy glimpses. Sightings, with cruel aftermaths – especially for Sylvie. Stevie has never asked but he knows there's a connection between addiction and the long line of watermen Grace married into. And he knows that, just as her mother has been driven away by her affiliation with the Tyler family, Ellie's life is just as intricately tied to the murky history of the sand and silt of the region.

He knows his story begins here but does not end here. He knows his story only briefly intersects with Ellie's. He knows his story is not about sand.

But this here, this small book in his hands – this is a piece of Ellie's history, her family, her heart. And now it's his.

"But this is your granddad's – your dad's. Yours." Stevie's throat catches.

Ellie shrugs. "You like to read."

Stevie suddenly feels himself spinning out from the tight circle they've all occupied for years. With one small breath, Ellie can pull him in and hold him close, but this is not Ellie reeling him back; this is a release, a gentle push. He feels the tenderness of this moment, this book: Ellie saying *go*, even as she draws a tentative line between their two paths, his course set for points beyond the wide mouth of the Chesapeake, hers standing firm on the ever-shifting silt of this mid-Atlantic region. He is sad and also grateful. He will cart this book with him the rest of his life. He will read it and re-read it and he'll even come back to the Chesapeake from time to time. He will carry Ellie's history with him, always. And he will be connected to it, too. But he will keep spinning outward, away, away.

"Come on," Ellie says, "let's go find some soft-shells."

§

They collect Manny and Sylvie from the beach and walk down the street to a pub where they sit at a long table covered in paper and order a half-bushel of jumbo crabs and two soft-shell sandwiches. Large glasses of lemonade, too. It's a hot September day and the mid-afternoon meal is succulent and sweet. Stevie bites into the white bread holding his soft-shell crab, sautéed just right, butter oozing, the tomato and lettuce and small dollop of tartar sauce exactly as they should be. Manny is handing over his crablegs to Sylvie, who is pounding them with vigor, the mallet large in her small hands.

Sylvie stops her banging and produces a small bottle from her backpack. She hands it across the table to Stevie.

"What's this?"

"Something from here," she says. It's not lost on Stevie that both sisters speak the same way, but Sylvie doesn't hold her heart; instead, she thrusts the bottle into his hand and laughs.

The bottle has a stopper cork and is filled with layers of color: grey, pink, black, even red, with a lighter shade of yellow on top. There are a few objects suspended among the grains, too, and a neatly tied yellow ribbon around the neck.

Stevie raises an eyebrow toward Ellie, who is sitting next to her sister. Manny leans in beside Stevie to look closer. Sylvie explains.

"The grey is the dirt from our back yard, near where we buried Yellow Bird." Stevie recalls the day they buried her canary together – his first introduction to this new friend.

"The shark's tooth is from Calvert Cliffs, where Ellie took me on my birthday. And the black is from the soil on the side of the house, where we plant our tomatoes. We add coffee grounds. They grow better that way. I love tomatoes."

Stevie and Ellie exchange smiles.

"The red is from Grandpa Harry's yard, in North Carolina. There's a tire swing in the tree. I have a box of dirt from there in my closet."

"I have weird shit in my closet, too," says Manny – an act of solidarity with the small child, but Stevie pokes him to shut up.

Sylvie ignores them both and continues, "The shells are from the last time I came to the beach, and the yellow – that's from today: sand."

Stevie chokes up, slugs his lemonade. Manny turns over his fifth crab to begin picking out the meat, and Ellie puts her arm around Sylvie.

Stevie is thinking of what to say when the bottle slips from his hand and drops. The cork pops off and the bottle rolls across the hardwood floor, its contents spilling out. It rolls further into the aisle, just as the waiter walks towards their table. In a moment of bad timing, the waiter steps on the bottle and it shatters.

Now Stevie's on his knees trying to re-shape the mess into a neat pile. He drags the edges of his hands together, cupping the sand and dirt. The layers are mixed now, the neat striations jumbled in a pile. He picks out shards of glass and scoops up some of it to bring back to the table, where the others sit dumbstruck by the misfortune.

"Shit, man, bad luck," says Manny, and Stevie is grateful that his friend has broken the silence because he's not sure what he would do with tears from either Ellie or Sylvie.

"Well, I got some of it."

Stevie hopes he can save the moment, say something meaningful to Sylvie. He glances at her, this small careful girl who has given him such a compact piece of her own story. He thinks she is pouting and refusing to look up at

68

him when he realizes she is rummaging in the backpack in her lap. She produces a small bottle – one exactly like the one she so carefully filled for him, only this one is empty.

"Here." She uncorks the bottle and holds it out across the table.

Stevie clumsily sifts the dirt and sand through his fingers into the small neck of the bottle. Some goes in, but most of it falls onto the table. It's a small drab thing when he holds it up to examine it. Half full. He shoves the shark's tooth and some of the small shells on top and corks it.

"Sorry," he finally says.

"That's OK," says Sylvie, pulling on her braid. "I know where there's more sand."

Dirty Martinis

by Len Kuntz

I'm not broke, but I'm getting there. Besides, it's lonely on the road and strangers are never as friendly as you'd guess.

So I pull over at a truck stop near Nashville with a *Help Wanted* sign in the window. It's a bartending gig, something I know a little something about having spent my last year of college fixing drinks for drunk frat boys at a strip club called *Jiggles*. The manager here is an obese man who goes by the moniker Hercules. He's so huge that it's torture for him to breathe and any time he moves or even leans a little it's like hearing a vacuum cleaner going full blast.

Herc gives me a test run. He has me make an Old Fashioned, a Manhattan, Dirty Martinis and even a Dirty Girl Scout, which, by the grin on his face, would be his trump recipe, yet I nail the concoction with just the right amount of Bailey's and a dash of crème de menthe. The happy smirk on his face tells me he's impressed.

"Start now if you want," Herc says.

I work my shift and another late into the evening. Herc is low on bartenders, I learn, because almost all of them end up stealing from the till, which is pretty stupid since there are two low-hanging cameras in each corner.

No one ever orders a Dirty Martini, let alone a Dirty Girl Scout. Mostly it's gin and tonics, whiskey straight up no ice, or rum and cokes. And beer of course. Lots of beer.

I try to keep things clean in and around my work space but there's so much alcohol soaked through the floorboards after all these years that certain spots give up a tight squeal when you step there, like crushing a poor kitten, plus the air smells like a well-used urinal.

The patrons are mostly miserable, and they're all drifters, yet an hour before midnight a lady comes in and I feel my knees buckle.

She looks exactly like my wife, but with red hair.

"Hey there," she says.

I try to speak but I've got rocks in my throat.

She takes the center stool at the bar, staring at me, daring me to look away. For a minute we just look at each other. I feel sweat dripping down my ribs. My socks are damp with sweat as well.

"Do I know you?" she finally says.

I swallow and manage to say, "I'm not from around here."

"Me either."

She smiles and it's my wife's smile, the kind she'd give me when she was in the mood for some hanky-panky.

"What'll it be?" I say, feeling dizzy and out of sorts.

"Give me your best drink, you pick."

So I make her a Dirty Martini and when she says, "Why don't you join me?" I do as she suggests, making another for myself. It's late and there's no one else in the place, plus I'm thirsty and nervous, needing something to take the edge off.

When we clink glasses in a toast, she says, "To chance encounters."

I drain my glass in three quick swallows. She flashes that smile again. I make another drink and try not to down it all at once.

She says, "You look like someone who's had their heart broken in a million pieces."

"How do you know that?"

"Ah, so you have?"

I nod. It feels like there's a balloon swelling in my chest. Since I left home, I've done a pretty adequate job of not thinking about my wife, but now, here with this woman who looks and acts so much like her, nostalgia ensnares me and I feel as weak and defeated as I did when I found out she was cheating on me.

"Hey now, it's all right," the woman says, reaching across the counter and clutching my hand which is damp with what I now realize are my own tears. "It's like they say: Time heals all wounds."

"You think?"

"There are plenty of fish in the sea," she says, using her free hand to unbutton her blouse.

"Hey."

"Momma said there'd be days like this."

"What are you doing?"

She draws my hand across the counter and pushes it inside her bra, purring, "There's no place like home."

Her skin is creamy and warm, her nipple as rigid as an eraser.

I reach under her armpits and hoist her off the stool and onto the bar counter, climbing on it too, positioning myself between her wide open thighs.

As I enter her, she grabs a fistful of my hair and yanks my head to hers, biting my ear, saying, "A stitch in time saves nine."

We go at it furiously. She makes the same urgent, wounded animal noises my wife would always make. She's demanding. She bites my other ear.

It lasts a half hour or an entire day, I can't be sure, because I'm in a netherworld. Everything feels right and somehow restored. When I say, "I've missed you so much," there's a guy across the bar in hunting fatigues sucking on a toothpick who snarls, calls me a "Queer" and backs out of the bar.

I look around for the woman who resembles my wife, but she's not there. I'm leaning over the bar, fully clothed. The air smells of jasmine, the fragrance my wife loved, or maybe it doesn't smell like anything other than barley and hops.

Ninth Inning

by Michael Webb

I have to get away. The team, like so many do, has descended into backbiting and innuendo, the blame circulating like bad air on a plane. The manager overmanages, the pitchers over-throw, the hitters overswing, and 4 straight losses becomes dropping 8 of 10 and the thin reed of your playoff hopes snaps off entirely. We are playing out the string in Baltimore, games that no one cares about under leaden skies, obeying the dictates of the schedule before small, unhappy crowds.

After a dismal 8-1 shellacking, which I was no small part of, and a tense phone call from Angela about behavior problems from the kids and my wavering interest in another baby, I decide I need to get out. I walk far enough from the hotel that I shouldn't be found, stepping into a mostly empty chain restaurant for a beer and some appetizers.

I was trying not to look at the lowlights of the Oriole hitters beating me like a rented mule on the televisions overhead, staring at the bubbles in my beer, when I feel her presence next to me.

"Hey stranger," she says. It is Jen, the reporter from Comcast, the only member of the press corps I remotely get along with. She is dressed up, expensive looking black pants, tall heels, and a thin, low cut top. Not altogether different from work attire, but with a little more sparkle. Like she is trying 20% harder to look good.

"Oh Jesus, not you," I say with mock seriousness. "I didn't give you enough this afternoon?"

"Hey," she says, taking a step back. "I'm off duty. Promise."

"Alright," I say, trying to sound gruff.

"May I join you?"

"Of course," I say.

The bartender, a chunky blonde with a purple streak on the side of her head, brings me my wings. Jen orders a beer for herself. I watch her cross her legs, the leather of her shoe reflecting the too bright lights. Overhead, I glance at myself as I wind and throw and watch a triple fly into the right field corner. When you get hit hard, the home media delights in your misery.

"Drowning your sorrows?" Jen says softly. Her makeup is quiet, professional, but expressive, a little flashier than usual. She is pretty, with the wide, oversized eyes of someone who is at home in front of a camera. I realize that I've seen more of her in the last month than I have of Angela, and I don't have the first idea of her personal life.

"You saw it," I say flatly. "I was shitty. What do you think?"

"Yeah," she says. "Your slider was flat, and your heater had no life. You're not hurt, are you?"

My back tenses, as if her saying the word can summon an injury. "I thought you were off duty!" I say with mock seriousness.

"Sorry," she says. She looks away, across the bar. "Force of habit."

"What sorrows are you drowning?" I ask.

"Me? Oh. I was meeting an ESPN producer here, but they are ..." she says, looking around for a clock, "seventy-five minutes late."

"For work?"

"Oh, no," she says, shaking her head.

"Oh," I say teasingly. "A hot date!"

"You could say that," she says. She looks away, her eyes wandering towards the door. A flush spreads down her neck. I can see the flat expanse above her cleavage turning pink. I feel the distance from home and Angela and Madison and Dylan, suddenly, silently aware of the 3000 miles that feel like ten million. I try to picture Jen in a single hotel room, undressing for bed, her shoes lonely and useless on a tan carpet. Something clicks inside me, Angela's biting anger on the phone and the smell of hot wings suddenly making me flush in sympathy with her.

"Anyone who would stand you up is a damn fool," I say. She is still looking at the door, the twisting emphasizing her trim waist and firm breasts as the blouse pulls taut. She turns back to look at me, her eyes slightly wet, her face softening into a smile.

"Thanks," she says softly. "That's nice to hear."

"So what's plan B for you?" I ask.

"This," she says. She smiles a little wider. She is half turned towards me in the chair.

"I'll drink to that," I agree. We clink glasses. A fat man in a Ravens cap across the bar from us looks up at the sound. An idea is forming at the base of my skull.

We drink in silence for a moment. The TV above our head shows the Orioles celebrating after their win, then a glimpse of a Raven at practice. I pick up a chicken wing and gnaw some of the meat off of it. I taste the grease and the bite of the spices. My eyes water.

"So what about after," I say, trying to sound casual. My heart pounds slightly. It's against all the codes of both of our professions, but the need tugs at me. Angela is a moon circulating a distant star, and Jen is here, and real, her bare, elegant calf inches from my skin. I can picture it. I want it.

"Oh, just bed," she says. She takes another long draft from her beer. "I don't have time to go out trawling." She is looking down again. You don't have to look far, I think at her. I'm right here. Jen finishes her beer and tugs at her pants, dusting off imaginary crumbs, preparing to stand. I look at her anxiously, trying to drain my own glass. She is fishing in a small leather clutch.

I stand. "Oh no," I tell her. "Let me," I say. "I make more money than you do."

"Oh," she says with surprise. I take out a credit card and lay it down, and the punk rock barmaid scoops it up like a carnivore on the savannah.

"Walk back with me?" I suggest.

"OK," she says. "Sure. We just can't go in together, you know?"

I understand. A group of professional athletes can gossip as well as any 7th grade class.

The barmaid comes back with the receipt, which I sign, adding a generous tip, and hand back. We walk towards the door. I don't know how to ask for her room number. Or will she ask for mine?

"Whoever he is," I say, holding the door as she makes her way into the September cool, "he's an idiot for standing you up this way."

"Yes," Jen says, the door shutting behind us. "She is."

High and Dry as Those Trapped Souls

by James Claffey

The top of the house overlooks the river and the surrounding countryside, and the Bird, as he sweeps the binoculars across the horizon, can name the neighbors who once were friends of his parents.

From his perch he can see across the tops of the houses to the distant farms: Hunt's, Lambert's, Delaney's, Keogh's, Mulvihall's, and Partridge's, all small farmers with ordinary cottages set in fine pastureland. When he was a boy his father and grandfather rowed across the fields to the houses cut off from the town by the overflowing river. His mother, one time, scanned the view for a sign of her husband and his father, who had taken Christmas packages to the isolated farmers, all trapped in their homes for weeks due to the terrific flooding that came like a Biblical plague at the end of one cold November.

"Where are you now, Mammy?" the Bird asks, the sun so strong his eyes are barely open. The room is mute, not even a spider moving in its web. "Ye've left me as high and dry as those trapped souls all those years ago," he says, wiping his watery eyes with a sleeve. Below, the CIE bus from Dublin pulls in and disgorges its passengers. Hard to make out, but the Bird knows by outline the names of a fair few of the passengers. It's been a long spell since he's had a day in Dublin, and he imagines taking a walk to the Long

Hall on South Great George's Street for as fine a pint as there is in Christendom.

A woman steps off the bus and holds her hand to her head, keeping her hat in place as the wind whips at her. Familiar frame. Ah, it couldn't be, he thinks. Melodie. Her height. Maybe even her hair, though he can't make out the shade, but the length is close. He throws the binoculars on the bed and flings himself towards the stairs. As he skitters down the staircase he feels the thump of his heart and says a quick Our Father that she's back in town. "Please God, let my luck be on the turn," he says, blessing himself before throwing open the front door and racing towards the bus stop.

At the stop, Melodie is arm-in-arm with one of the musicians from the band she played with the night he first saw her in Hogan's. A tinny feeling comes over the Bird and he totters backwards and almost trips over the leg of a chair. His chest is hollow, lacking in blood, and he slumps to a sitting position on a wooden bench by the window of Grace's Butcher's shop. Her name sticks in his craw and he unscrews the flask in his pocket and gulps down a mouthful of the burning drink. "Me ... Melo ..." he can't form the syllables of her name and simply witnesses the bastard kiss her hard on the mouth. The Bird retreats to the steps outside his house, the nun's house, and drains the flask in one go.

Inside, in the kitchen, he takes the plates drying on the table and holds them above his head.

"One for sorrow ..."

Crash.

"Two for joy ..."

Crash.

"Three for a girl ..."

Crash.

"Fecking hoor ..."

The last plate explodes on the linoleum floor and bits of china litter the place like confetti. Through the settings of bone china the Bird laments his lost love, sure that the man she is with cannot possibly give her anything like the attention he would. These are the dishes he pictured her filling with delicious French cooking, her hair pinned back in a bow, the apron tight about her waist, his little woman making their lovely home together.

"Bitch. Bitch. Bitch."

He yells so the windows shake and the nuns might hear his cries, but he doesn't give a fig for their reverence. More bitches, too, those bloody nuns and their insistence of not allowing their converts to choose their path in religious life.

The kitchen he leaves like a madhouse, the shards of china everywhere, the possibility of love shattered into so many impossible pieces as they send his heart straight to hell. In the bedroom the wardrobe door rattles and he shakes a head at such madness. "Leave me alone, Mother," he cries. "Go back to hell and leave me to this misery." The door opens and his mother leaps out and in a jiffy he's across the floor scooting his entire body into the relative safety of the nearby corner. "Bird, Bird, Bird. You soft touch. Didn't I tell you all women would be your downfall?"

"No, Mother! You promised me happiness. You promised me a life to enjoy, you vicious traitor."

The mother clucks and beckons him forward. "Filthy. You disgusting creature!"

He raises his eyebrows and summons up a mouthful of spit, which he gullies into her ghostly figure. Nothing. No response. Not even a "Goodness!" Instead of disgust, the creature folds in on herself and in moments is gone. The Bird cries as he beats his fists on the door of the wardrobe. All love is pointless, he thinks. The wardrobe door shakes and trembles, the curses stored by him for some time now fly from his lips as he directs his anger and hatred towards the remaining actors and stage people.

Misery loves company, and the Bird wishes he had the company of someone to drown his sorrows. He thinks a trip to McKettrick's might reveal Melodie and her musical lover, and he doesn't give a damn. If he gets the chance he'll let her know exactly who he thinks she is, in no uncertain terms. Yet, he knows this is a lie, and that he'll end up toasting her happiness and bemoaning his useless religion, which only seems to satisfy the people around him, and never himself.

Before he sets out for the pub he descends to the back storage room outside the kitchen. There he grabs several ancient planks of wood and a handful of nails. With the hammer firmly in his grasp, he bangs the planks across the wardrobe door, the nails splintering the polished wood of the piece. Each swing of the hammer brings another curse out of his mouth. "Rot. In. Hell. You. Dirty. Fecker." He swings the last hammer blow so hard the head of the tool disappears into the wooden splinters, opening the wardrobe for surreptitious viewing.

"Now, then. You trollop of a Frenchwoman, it's time I set my intention, once and for all." The door slam must rattle the windows of the entire town, for the barking of dogs and the mewing of cats fill the evening with plainsong.

Wednesday

17

September
2014

My Suicide,
Interrupted

by Gwendolyn Joyce Mintz

Mora will be angry. But I believe at some point she'll understand. I can't text that goodbye and certainly not to her. She's a glimmer of hope that won't die out. Why I love her. And why I don't trust her. She might call or text back and then what – my suicide interrupted?

Phone's off. Neither she nor the others can call or text to see why I'm not at the meeting.

It's time. It's time. It's past time.

It may take them a minute to understand why Lindsey arrives at the table with the glasses but I hope they smile when she tells them I made arrangements earlier and tonight the champagne's on me.

Undone

by Stephen V. Ramey

"Control-Z," I say. *Undo last change.* "Remember how I showed you?"

Frank leans over the keyboard. I lean over his shoulder. I've been trying to teach him Microsoft Excel for a couple of weeks now. He got it in his head to do his household budget on the computer though he thinks it's a magic box with evil intentions. His daughter bought it for him last Christmas.

A stream of "z" stretches through several cells.

"You have to push the keys at the same time, Frank." I reach past him. "Here, let me show –"

"No, no, I'll get it." He positions his left index finger precisely over the *Ctrl* key, his right over *Z* and mashes both down. The river of "z" disappears, followed by the mistake and the correct entry he made before it.

He lifts his hands, triumphant.

"Nice," I say, "only you don't have to hold the keys down so long. See how it erased the Mortgage amount too?"

Frank chuckles. "I wish it were that easy."

"There's a way to redo that," I say, but he's already pecking keys on the number pad.

"That works too."

Frank is an interesting fellow. He's reserved most of the time, but when he's hooked on a topic or focused on a task, he can be like a bulldog. Fortunately, we made a gentleman's agreement my first day here that we would not pry into each other's lives. Frank may be tenacious, but he respects a bond as much as any man I have met. I like him a lot.

We've come to depend on each other. I drive him to the grocery store and mow the lawn and he lets me use his computer for the draft of my novel. He knows I'm writing, but has yet to ask what or why I write so late at night.

I'm up to chapter seven and feeling pretty good. I do miss Anne, especially in the mornings. She used to brew coffee before she went to work and would leave a note reminding me of whatever needed reminding that day. I loved the way she signed *Anne* with a flourish, that final swoop leaping up into the text of the note. I loved Anne. I think I still do, but that must be wrong. How could I give her up so easily if my love was true? Cold turkey is for quitting drugs, not emotional involvement.

I feel healthier since I came to stay with Frank. Mostly it's the lessened stress, I imagine. I used to worry every night that Anne would hate me for letting her down, or obsess over what new horror the doctors would find. I still remember word for word the call in which Dad told me his cancer had relapsed. He'd been on an experimental regimen and the tumors were shrinking. Hope had resurfaced; I heard it in his voice, saw it in his eyes. And then, "It's back." A sigh. The liver tumor had expanded and a second emerged. *Inoperable.* "What about a transplant?" "It's in my stomach and lymphs." And though we talked a few times after that, that was the goodbye I remember, the exhaustion in his voice. "Love you, Dad," I said. "Make me proud," he said. A choke, a click, and life would never be the same.

"Did I do that right?" Frank says. He's pointing at a cell in the spreadsheet that shows $742.35. The cells above it are encased in a solid border, indicating they are included in the summation.

"That's perfect, Frank." I pat his shoulder and his face breaks into a smile.

"I guess it's never too late," he says.

"For what?" I'm thinking of Dad's profile against a glowing television screen. *His face is so thin.*

"It's never too late to see the light," Frank says.

My throat seizes up. Dad used to say something like that. *Hang in there, Son. It's never too late to learn the dance.* He'd say that when I confided that life was not so good, another rejection, Anne on the warpath, a failed attempt to install a bathroom ceiling fan. *Don't let the world shut you down,* he'd tell me. *You'll find your music, I know you will.*

We were never close until he got sick. I'd seen him as an ineffective authority figure, someone to ignore, even mock. The illness made things right between us, gave me the relationship I had (unknowingly) craved.

And then it took him down. *Cancer. Death.* Every wise thing he'd told me was lost to my heart, every ounce of love destroyed. He *was* weak; a stronger man would have lived, a truer father would have seen our healing complete.

The computer screen blinks off. Frank's chair pushes back. I move. Air resists me; I hear a river rushing. My hands curl into fists. My eyes find the keyboard, the keys *Ctrl* and *Z*. Index fingers extend.

"How's spaghetti for tonight?" Frank squeezes my shoulder and moves past me to the kitchen.

"Fine," I say, but it's another voice I hear. *Make me proud, Son.*

Guilt

by Gay Degani

Dr. Sam Martin finds himself on the sidewalk along the Old
Road, his mind a jagged mosaic: the breeze smelling of
barbeque – the days getting shorter – he should get rid of
that stack of wood – why hasn't that stop sign, twisted by
last January's windstorm, been replaced? And then, an
image of Charmaine, hands on hips, belly beginning to
swell – Charmaine smashing the new tile in the bathroom –
Charmaine curled next to their aero-bed, her nightgown
crumpled above her waist, the worn pine floor stained with
blood. Why is he out here in front of his house on the
wrong side of the gate with some old man poking him in
the chest, raising his voice, "Hey, Doc! Doc?"

Frowning, Sam asks, "W-why are you shouting at me?"

"You okay, Doc?"

"Me? I'm fine – fine."

"You don't look fine."

Sam hones in on the old guy, then studies his dog. Al?
Fred? Gus! The dog is Gus? No, the old *man* is Gus, the
same one who helped him search the Trencher mansion for
Charmaine. Sam says, "Gus, right? And Gracie?"

"No one forgets Gracie. Any news?"

When Sam reported his wife missing two months ago,
after turning the neighborhood upside down, the cops
asked if the remodeling was causing any stress, were they
getting along okay, did she have a temper, did he have a

temper? He explained the miscarriage and his wife's depression, and the older cop, the one with the bad hair plugs, muttered, "Uh-huh," in that cynical way people do. Sam felt guilty then. He still feels guilty now. Whatever happened to Charmaine, he should have kept her safe, helped her cope. It was his fault. He hadn't handled anything right when she lost the baby. When *they* lost the baby.

"Doc!"

"Sorry. Just can't remember why I came outside. You know the feeling."

"Not me." Gus taps his own forehead. "Mind like a steel trap. You know what strikes me is that we had someone at the bungalow disappear too. The night of the storm."

The line between Sam's brows deepens.

"Yeah," says the old man. "Not like your wife exactly because this one left with her two kids. Her husband was, well, what we used to call a wife-beater, at least according to Sybil, our landlady. Jamie was her name, packed her suitcase and when the storm happened, she took off."

"Charmaine wouldn't leave me, not like that. We – I'm not – like him."

"Oh, I didn't mean that. The thing is, after she left, she never called Sybil. They were close, so it's kind of surprising. And Jamie didn't take her suitcase. It got crushed by the oak when it landed on her house. Sybil's storing all her stuff in the garage."

Sam remembers the fallen tree. It had taken months to get the whole mess cleaned up and now it doesn't look like the bungalow is going to be rebuilt. "No one ever heard from her?"

"That's what I mean. Sybil still has her cleaning deposit too. You'd think she'd need the money if not her stuff. You haven't heard from your wife either, right?"

Flashes from the day Charmaine flipped out, taking a hammer to their bathroom, and hiding in the nursery of the deserted Trencher mansion next door kaleidoscope through Sam's mind. He pivots slowly toward the big Mediterranean looming over its unkempt yard. When she disappeared a few months later, he was certain that's where she'd gone, but she hadn't.

Gus yammers on. "... two women disappearing on the same street, but she'll be okay, Doc. You know how women are. Right, Gracie?" The old man tugs at the dog's leash, and the mutt cocks her head. "We gotta get going, don't we, girl? Keep the home fires burning, Doc. She'll be back."

Without another word, Gus turns and limps across the Old Road and taking the path down to the creek, he disappears into the growing dusk.

Sam deflates as if Gus's arthritic finger had left a pinhole in his chest. The gloom thins him almost to nothing, a thought, a vapor, the memory of a vapor. He plucks at memory and finds only fading shards. An early autumn chill prickles his neck as he steps toward the mansion.

After he'd reported Charmaine's disappearance, the police searched their house and because Sam claimed he'd gone inside the Trencher mansion to search for his wife, they'd searched that too. They knew the old man had gone inside with him and they'd scared away a squatter, some kid. Sam said it hadn't been his wife, and they believed him.

The window that had been his way in when he'd looked for Charmaine the day she disappeared, is locked. He uses his elbow to break the glass, not hearing its shattering sound against the evening quiet. He has to do this again, compelled to get into this house, doomed to repeat this experience over and over just to make sure she isn't waiting inside for him to find her. To take her home. To make another baby. To give him another chance.

Knocking away the remaining shards of the pane, Sam barely feels the sting of sliced skin as his hand rakes across a tooth of glass. Blood gushes warm, but he ignores it, reaching in to unlock the window, sliding it up. He hesitates, almost overwhelmed by what he knows is futility, but then he sighs and hoists himself up, puts a foot onto the sill, then heaves his torso through the opening, dragging his other leg behind. He falls inside, landing hard on his knees and hands. The scream, he thinks, is coming from deep inside his own chest, syncopating with the drumming in his ears. Pain shoots through his bloody injured palm, up his arm. He curls head to knees, cradling his hand, and in the new silence, he understands it isn't he who screamed.

He struggles to stand, the gloomy house spinning around him. He bellows, "Hey, who's here?"

The grim absolute silence of the house seeps into him, the smell of moldy decay. He pivots around toward the window, a muddy green square behind him, dusk coming on. And beyond the window he hears shouts and voices. And then as if suddenly compelled, the feeling of urgency sinking into his crotch, he leaps into the hall, into the kitchen, and throws open the bolt on the back door and heads out, circling the old mansion into the front.

Glimpsing his own weedy yard, he hardly recognizes it, distorted by shadows, a foreign landscape. Someone hollers, a dog barks, a mumble of voices, and as he swings around, figures move out onto the sidewalk, huddled together, and then in the distance, a siren sounds. Sam strides toward the crowd. A woman in some kind of a caftan turns toward him as he approaches and behind her, he spies someone sitting on the curb, the old man, Gus, his dog yapping.

"What happened?" Sam says. "Is he hurt?"

"No," answers the woman. She grasps his arm tight. "He found a – body – creek."

"What do you mean?" he asks, thinking dog, coyote, maybe a horse? There's a horse trail along the creek.

Streetlights flick on and he can see the woman's frightened face. He recognizes her as the owner of the bungalows. Her fingernails dig through his shirt.

Connections

by Sally-Anne Macomber

To: Milton Flaxmill, Red Cow Publishing
From: Trudy Polaris
Date: September 20, 2014 1:07 p.m.
Re: Do you know any fashion designers?

Dearest Milton,

We had some strange visitors yesterday.

At first I thought they were spies.

It was about 11.33am and I heard a knock on the door of our Tyrolean hideaway. I thought it might be one of the goats playing a practical joke, knocking on the door, and then I thought, no, wait a minute, if it was one of the goats I would have heard hooves on the stairs and the bell around its neck, ringing with each step.

"I think there's someone at the door," I said to my husband.

He looked up from the crossword in the *Kitzbuheler Anzeiger* and said, "So open the fucking door!" (Such a kidder, my husband.)

I opened the door and there on the doorstep stood a tall, thin man with a clipped moustache and wearing a blue and yellow t-shirt.

This is not such a strange thing, though, finding a tall, thin man with a clipped moustache and wearing a blue and yellow t-shirt standing on your doorstep. This happens a lot here in the Tyrol, usually tourists losing their way and wanting to know directions to the nearest Autobahn or skiers who took a wrong turn back in March still trying to locate the nearest piste or locals wanting to see for themselves the woman who almost bankrupted the local dairy industry with her wheeling and dealing in Bulgarian feta.

(Grooooaaan! Yes, the gossip still continues. Tyrolean dairy farmers have a loooong and unforgiving memory.)

The strange thing is, he started talking to me in English. Like he expected me to know English. "I am looking for the nearest Autobahn," he said, with not a trace of a Swedish accent. "We are lost."

He held a map in his hand and being the super-friendly person I am – I was, after all, voted *Person Most Likely to Give You Helpful Advice When You Are Lost on a Fishing Trip* at high school – I pointed out to him where we are on the map and where the nearest Autobahn is. He thanked me, still no trace of a Swedish accent, and then walked back to his car.

"I think they're spies," I said to my husband, as I sat in the window and watched the car (it had Swedish plates) still parked on the side of the goat track. The man was talking to his companion – well, I assume they were companions, unless they were both looking for the nearest Autobahn and had somehow, through extreme luck, met each other and discovered they were both lost in the very same way.

Soon I was slithering along the ground in my goat-milking uniform (industrial-strength leather apron and matching vinylette overalls), as these are the only real outdoor clothes I own, so I could spy on them. I wedged a stale slice of feta under one of the back wheels of the car with the Swedish plates – they still hadn't caught sight of me! And luckily for me, I have been inventing lightweight but durable building bricks out of the old Bulgarian feta we have just laying around the front yard – and with the impromptu tin cans attached with string I had made on a whim just that very morning (you forget I'm a scientist, Milton, my mind must be occupied with *something* while I wait to hear from you!), I pressed one against the back passenger door and listened with the other.

I couldn't make out much of their conversation, but the two words I did manage to hear were 'Prize' and 'Oslo'. So I can only assume I am being awarded the Nobel Prize!

I did not hear the words 'Literature' or 'Physics' but I am sure the prize will be awarded to me for one of them. When I find out, you will be the first (after my husband) to know.

After the tall, thin man with the clipped moustache and wearing the blue and yellow t-shirt stopped talking to his companion, he started the car's ignition and drove off in a cloud of dust (even I was surprised by how dusty the cloud was!) and I was left by the side of the road holding the can.

This will be great for publicity for the book. The latest bestseller from Red Cow Publishing, written by a Nobel Prize winner!

So now I am wondering if Red Cow Publishing has any productive connections with Scandinavian fashion designers. I am thinking a dress made of silvery-yellowish white, to represent nuclear fission, would be best, though I realise this is an unusual colour and perhaps not every fashion designer can work with such a distinctive shade.

Have you been to one of these events before, Milton? The Queen of Sweden attends and it is usually held on December 10th, so there is still some time (though not a lot) to have the dress designed and ready for my appearance in Oslo. (I read this on Wikipedia, about the dates and the venue.) And I'm sure most fashion designers would love to design the gown of the next winner of the Nobel Prize for Literature and / or Physics.

Is there some protocol for who I should thank at the publishing house? I know I have a tendency to rush things in social situations but you probably have a list of thankees your authors should thank on important occasions like this.

As always, looking forward to your reply,

Trudy Polaris.

To: Leonard Strauss Jr., Red Cow Publishing
From: Trudy Polaris
Date: September 20, 2014 3:52 p.m.
Re: Scandinavia

Dear Herr Strauss Jr.,

Even though I have not heard from you, I *do* have some big news! I can't say yet just exactly what it is, as I wish to avoid a Tyrolean media stoush.

(The locals here are so disapproving of attention-seeking behaviour and while your sister seems like a sweet old Frau – I mean, when she's not clearly avoiding me. There are, after all, only so many Tyrolean beech trees she can hide behind! – I can't guarantee that if I tell you and you tell her, she won't rush off and tell the science columnist at the *Kitzbuheler Anzeiger* and then *everyone* will know.)

But what I can tell you is it involves a glamorous dress, foreign dignitaries, the social whirl of Scandinavian academia and a big gold gong.

More soon,

Frau Trudi von Polarissen

To: Boy Polaris
From: Trudy Polaris
Date: September 20, 2014 8:27 p.m.
Re: your internship at Red Cow Publishing

If Leonard Strauss Jr. hasn't noticed you by now and given you your own desk and maybe even your own locker, it's probably because you're not wheeling down the corridors of Red Cow Publishing fast enough, making yourself visible.

And how can he give you a contract to sign if he's never clapped eyes on you?!

Put yellow highlights in your blue hair and double your whey powder protein shakes to build up your biceps so you'll roll down the corridors of Red Cow Publishing in your wheelchair quicker.

Otherwise, my only other advice is, suck it up princess!

Your loving mother

One Way or Another

by Mandy Nicol

Charlie and I went to Angela's wedding yesterday. Angela looked beautiful, in a sheathed mermaid type of way. She confided she had stacked on the kilos this past fortnight while fretting over whether she's doing the right thing, whether she really wants to settle down and live the rest of her life with one person.

It might have been that last comment or it might have been too much champagne but later, after the reception, something made me say yes to Charlie.

And so I had to tell Mum.

Mum is sitting opposite me at the dining table, glaring at the chocolate éclair I've placed in front of her. Seph sits on her knee, entranced, trying to inhale the éclair with her tiny busy nostrils.

I sip my coffee then say, "It's really not that bad."

Mum doesn't answer. Instead she reaches out to the plate, swipes a dollop of cream onto her fingers and offers it to Seph. The little pink tongue licks with rabid delicacy.

I want to throw my coffee at both of them.

"It's only three weeks, Mum. I haven't had a proper holiday since we all went to Wilsons Prom when Dad was still alive." God, that's twenty years ago.

Peregrine ambles over, sits down beside my chair and rests his head on my lap. I fondle his ears. I'd like to give him some of my vanilla slice but he's on a diet.

"I really don't understand what you're so upset about," I say.

Mum takes a deep, exaggerated, *it should be painfully obvious* breath and the dam breaks.

"I can't be trapped here all by myself for three weeks, Nadia. It's bad enough being here alone when you waltz off with Charlie for a weekend, and now you want to go away for three weeks? Anything could go wrong in three weeks. There could be a fire, or a power black-out and the generator won't work, I could fall over and hurt my hip again, or break a leg, an arm. My neck. There's the dogs to look after, and the chooks. What if there's a fire? What if the phone lines are down and I can't call for help? And what about bread? I'm not freezing bread, it's unnatural, and I can't very well make it …"

I glance at the breadmaker on the kitchen bench, shoved in a corner under a stack of recipe books and appliance manuals. I look back at Mum and she won't meet my eyes so I look at the breadmaker again, for a little longer, and watch her out of the corner of my eye. She lifts her gaze straight back to my face.

"… Well what about milk?" she continues. "You won't catch me drinking that long-life rubbish." She contorts her lips as if her head is in a bucket of rotten yoghurt. "No, three weeks is too long Nadia, it won't work. You can't go."

She picks up her éclair with her Seph-cleaned fingers.

I don't stop her.

I wait until she finishes eating, then I say, "I wasn't expecting you to stay here by yourself Mum. We're talking about December and Anthony said he'd be home from New York well before Christmas. If he isn't here you could go and stay with Celeste in Melbourne. Or Celeste and the kids could come and stay here. Or we could ask the neighbours to keep an eye on you and do some shopping for you. We'll work something out."

She stares at me.

I stare back.
And I say, "One way or another, I'm going."

Dr. Stanley
Has a Date

by Margaret Bingel

Nora's foot taps on the ground as she sits on the park bench. Even though there is no chill of autumn yet, she pulls on the sleeve of her blouse, fingers tracing the seam. I could leave now, she tells herself. I can just get up, and go, and pretend this didn't happen and I can go back home. A stranger's laugh tears her from her thoughts, and she whips her head over her shoulder nervously.

When her son told her to go out and find herself a man, what Nora couldn't tell him was that she already had man problems; Dr. Stanley had been courting her for weeks. Flowers every Saturday, and a weekly phone call every Wednesday, as well the occasional coffee date, leaves no question in Nora's mind about Dr. Stanley's ("Please, call me Rob," he told her back in June) intentions. But all the attention made Nora very suspicious about the universe's sudden interest in giving her a husband. Having never married, with only a son to love, Nora doesn't think she has the backbone to take another man's hand. Am I too old for a romance? Nora asks.

Dr. Rob Stanley approaches the park bench behind her, carrying two sacked lunches and a tray holding two coffees. He watches the bun perched low on her head, her hair a soft brown, like a mouse. If there are grays in her lovely hair, he thinks, it'll only suit to match her eyes. He sits down next to her, and she turns to face him. The sun on

Nora's face makes it shine like a golden medallion, and Rob has to catch his breath. She is so beautiful, he thinks, while he offers her a coffee.

Nora takes one of the lunch sacks instead and pulls out a turkey sandwich. Spying an apple and a small bag of chips, she looks up and smiles.

"Thank you for lunch, Rob. You even got me a green apple. How did you know I like green apples?"

"Well Nora, they're tart and sweet, just like you. And since birds of a feather ..." Rob's voice trails off, and his eyes squint in the sun. "Nora, does Ned have a dog?"

Now it's Nora's turn to hold her breath. She doesn't like him asking so many questions about her son. It makes her feel like she's holding secrets, and she has always shared everything with Ned.

"Yes. Nadia. Why do you ask?"

Rob notes the trepidation in her voice and her furrowed brow.

"He offered me a dog treat during one of our Wednesday sessions. I just wanted to make sure that he wasn't eating them himself. It was liver and cheese flavored."

Rob laughs, and Nora chuckles along with him. She thinks he looks handsome when he lets himself actually smile, and not just smirk at her. She reaches her hand over and grabs his, looking deep into his eyes.

From a distance, Ned watches his mother kiss his physical therapist. He knows Dr. Stanley saw him, walking along the path by the pond, and he'll have a little talk with him real soon.

Nadia nudges Ned's leg, and tightening his hold on her lead again, he walks away from the blossoming couple, a small grin creeping across his face.

Tuesday

23

September
2014

Big As Life

by Darryl Price

Hey. It's me. And I suppose by default it's you. Have I said that before? I've been feeling flat again lately. Like a piece of paper. Not part of any stack. We've talked about this before. I've been having a few thoughts going around like loosely rolling marbles racing past each other in my head lately. So I thought I'd run them by you. See if they're worth listening to.

Tell me, Doc, do we get to see the ones we loved again – the way they were when we loved them?

Will I feel anything when I'm gone?

Will I know myself?

I'm not sure where this line of questioning came from, it just came from somewhere, and it won't leave me alone, so I'm looking for an answer. Maybe that will help it find the front door, so to speak.

Hey, Doc, wait, did I tell you I met someone? At a bake sale of all places actually. It's an interesting story. At first all I heard was her voice, yeah I know not a good sign, but it attracted me, that sound. Turns out she was selling homemade cupcakes to raise money for something or other. They had pink icing on them, Doc, and it just turned something over inside me – that and her voice, which, if I may, sounded like a beautiful wild bird making happy noises in the highest branches of an extraordinarily beautiful blue sky kind of day. To me.

That about sums it up as far as the feelings go.

We started talking and she didn't run away and neither did I. We actually stayed in eye contact with each other in that moment in that room on purpose. It threw me for a loop, Doc. I thought I was pretty much all done with that sort of flirty thing, but you know what, Doc? It felt good. Natural. I liked her presence. It didn't scare me. Well, not right away.

Well, don't get me wrong – I hightailed it out of there pretty doggone quickly after that. I didn't want to ruin things right off the bat. But now get this, Doc, she'd written her phone number on the inside of the cake box flap. When I got home I decided to have a cupcake with a big old glass of milk and guess what, that's when I noticed it. Big as life. Hand-written. Like a beautiful ribbon.

I don't know. Maybe she writes that on every box top – to try to drum up business – but there was a smiling face next to it! And it said, "hope to see you again real soon."

Now that I think about it, it does seem a bit ambiguous.

Don't matter. I already called her up. We're going to go out to dinner some time. I didn't want to sound too anxious. I told her it would be likely pretty soon. Guess I can be just as ambiguous. Then all those questions started bothering me.

And so here we are. You and me. Like always. Together again. At least on paper. We are paper warriors of the heart, or is it worriers?

Are we friends, Doc? No, don't answer that – I don't want to know. Just help me if you can.

Stuck between a cupcake lady and a memory I can't ever forget.

Take a Leap

by Teresa Burns Gunther

It's Wednesday night. The days are shorting out to fall. The lights downtown are visible in my "view slice" through the houses across the street. My tea has gone cold in my surfing shark mug – a gift from my cousin, Susie. She followed Steve, Kevin's cousin, to LA and landed her dream job – a part in a daytime soap.

Susie's life is a minefield but she has a cellular abundance of hope. I have always stopped to analyze what's practical, doing what I want but making sure it makes sense. We both land on our feet but hers are more likely to end up in daisies.

I watch the last of the neighbors going in, collapsing strollers, dropping running shoes into front porch baskets, putting gardening tools away; the last car is jockeying for legal purchase before tomorrow's 6:00 a.m. street sweeping. So many lights and houses, all the lives that surround, but are so separate from mine. It used to make me lonely. But now I have Kevin. *And you,* I tell Stella and rub her with my foot, she moans and wags her tail.

It's hard to believe 2014 is 73.15% over.

Maybe it's the shark's teeth that remind me of another fall, when boys and possibilities for love seemed innumerable. I was 15, a junior in high school. My father dropped me off that day in his sports car, loud with rock music. His car attracted as many boys as my long legs in a short skirt. "You're a star," my father crowed as he sped off, the actor enjoying playing the rare role of father that morning.

Joey Markham was waiting in his leather jacket, leaning against the corner of the art building. His eyes were all over me. His curiosity was thrilling. As I drew closer I slowed down, setting one foot directly before the other. I looked right into his eyes, telling myself that I wasn't afraid of anyone, a mantra I repeated all the time.

He called me beautiful and I said *yes*.

He fell in step, checking me out from beneath his lank hair. "Yes, what?"

"You can take me out on Friday." I was glad for the bright sun that made him squint hoping he wouldn't see my heart rattling in my throat. He grinned and told me I was *something*.

He was a senior so I knew he'd expect more grown up activity than the boys I'd dated freshman year. On Friday, we went out for pizza and a movie. In the empty back of the theater, third row from the last, I let him touch my breasts, slide his hands under my panties, let him put my hand on his penis that was stiff and pointing at the screen. The sting of this pleasure fascinated me. *Next time*, I told him, when he asked for more. He took me to a party the following Friday night, and after serving me beer from a keg, after introducing me to his friends who were older, smoked pot and were more interesting than anyone from school, he pulled me into a back bedroom where posters of race cars and naked girls adorned the walls. This excited me, too. And I lay back, watching as he undressed me, ringing with titillation and desire and when he entered me I knew. On Monday he would tell all the kids at school.

Kevin thinks I'm something, too. He's what Gail, my officemate, calls a "mensch." He makes me believe in love and puts an X in most of the boxes on my man wish list. I'm smarter now. Stella is crazy about him and he likes her.

He's smart and kind, successful, he plays guitar and thinks I'm funny – funny good, not strange. Best of all he's tall! I believe things are *looking up! Ha Ha.*

My resolution for September is trust, take a *leap of faith.* Or as Susie would say: *take a walk on the spiritual side.* I'm not after any kooky-guru-lala-ram-das-crystals-incense trip, but something beyond the numbered, efficient order of my days. I've always been about fact and logic, my life ordered in black and white. I like a sharp pencil and a crisp lined pad where things add up. But as hard as I've tried to extend this calculus to my real life, it hasn't made the leap. Lives are hard to engineer. I'm trying to practice losing control, not an easy move for me. I want to know what it feels like to believe in the impossible, I want to stop making sense.

My phone buzzes with a text from Kevin, *b there in 2.* "Hmm ..." I sound the humming he sets off in me. It's scary to believe, with no other proof than how I feel inside. Scary because hope usually travels with its sad cousin: disappointment. I close my eyes, take a deep breath, I'm learning how to relax.

I hear his car whip around the corner and into my driveway. I watch him unfold from his car, all 6 foot 3 of him. Stella dashes down the steps, nearly knocking him over with her joy. He holds a pizza box high in the air and smiles up at me. He calls me *beautiful.* I call him *pizza man* and remind myself to just keep practicing letting things unfold without a plan.

Morgana Malone and the Mystery of the Secret Gift

by Matt Potter

"La Petite Fleurette Select Patisserie and Gifterie," I say into the receiver.

"Is that the Royal Rose Cake Shop?" a voice, sing-song wavery and uncertain, says on the end of the line. "I'm looking for the Royal Rose Cake Shop."

"Yes, we *were* the Royal Rose Cake Shop," I say, "we just have a new name. But it's the same service and we make the same cakes and we're at the same address."

"You haven't changed your range of cakes?" the older woman asks.

This happens two, three, seventeen times a day with Mum's old customers. And I curse Jane – my sister, who's still the new Susan (because I'm still the old Susan) – for changing the name of Mum's cake shop, hoping it will make the business more saleable when Mum decides to retire. Or when my sister decides it's time for Mum to retire.

I breathe in, and smell the sugary-sweetness of years of vanilla sponges and fruit cakes and cream puffs and lemon meringue pies and pavlovas.

"Oh good," the older woman sighs. "I always order a triple Victoria sponge for family birthdays and I need to order two. The family's getting so large now one triple Victoria sponge isn't enough."

I scribble *2 x triple Victoria sponges* and her name (which means nothing to me when she tells me but the way she says it, she obviously thinks it should) and her 'phone number on the order form – a newly-printed pad of them with the newly-minted *La Petite Fleurette Select Patisserie and Gifterie* at the top in pink curly-curly cursive – then tear if off the pad and place it in the *Orders – In* tray beside the 'phone. I want to ask her if, by *the family's getting so large*, she means in number or in size, but it's not always a good thing to ask a customer just how fat her family is, in case their weight *is* tipping the Richter scale.

"What's a *Gifterie*?" she says.

My face flushes and my armpits are suddenly sticky. I hate stammering the official "the *Gifterie* is an exclusive gift shop offering a select range of giftware." When instead I want to say *Hey, it's stocked with the stuff Jane / Susan ordered for her* NOT *Made in China shop that was accidentally made in China after all.*

So instead I say, "Thanks for your order," a little too loudly, and hang the 'phone back in its cradle.

And that's when I hear a voice, harsh enough to scratch glass on a rainy day. "I'm looking for Morgana Malone."

I step through the doorway, from the backroom into the main part of the shop, and sidle up to Mum behind the counter.

Mum's powdery face lights up, like she's forgotten I'm here. "There's someone to see you, love."

Mum's grey eyes are revealing … well, not a lot, really. What they *are* saying, is that she knows nothing of this woman. Who I see has long dyed-brown hair pulled off a face with no makeup, pulled back under a small blue headscarf. And is wearing a white blouse. And a longish skirt with small blue flowers spread across it. I don't know what she's wearing on her feet because I can't see over the counter but given the top half of her outfit, probably flat white sandals.

"Morgana!" she says.

And then I piece the voice and the blue eyes and the growing-back eyebrows together and realise that underneath the new hair and the 50's housewifey fashion statement it's –

"Zebadie," I say, clasping my hands behind my back.

I am *so* glad I'm standing behind the counter. Otherwise she'd rush over and throw her arms around me, pressing me against those massive ... my God, no wonder I didn't recognise her! Her three and a half boob jobs are gone too! She's been gutted, filleted, her breastwork lipo-suctioned out of her and replaced by something new. Or maybe something old.

Standing against the spring sun shining through the shop window, she's almost ... concave.

And then I remember the last time we met – the day of the wedding rehearsal when I was supposed to be her bridesmaid – she called me a *cunt*.

And I can't help it, it's so obvious I have to say something. And hand at my cleavage, "What happened to your –"

"Oh those old things," and Zebadie waves her hand in the air, like they're yesterday's news. "I had them refashioned after I got the hostess job on the Plymouth Brethren Home Shopping Network."

I'm about to say, *So once again you've used your breasts for a career move,* but instead, Mum draws herself up to her full height, which is just above my shoulder, and says, "So you're the one who called my daughter a *cunt*?!"

Zebadie smiles. "Look, I'm not here to talk about how cunty or how *un*cunty your daughter was," she says, "trying to steal my fiancé from on top of me the day before my wedding. But what I *am* here to tell you is that" – and here she pierces me with those blue blue eyes and I wonder, just *what* is she going to say now, when she says – "Grigor forgives you."

I stand there.

Just looking.

I don't know what to say.

It's not that I'm waiting for someone else to butt in – which is normal when my family is around – but my lips are dry and my armpits are sticky and my mouth opens and nothing comes out.

"He wants you to know that. And he's dropping all the charges against you, too," Zebadie adds.

"What *charges?*" Mum asks, eyes fierce and her chin indignant.

"Breach of promise and criminal intent to bankrupt," Zebadie recites, like she's reading off a charge sheet.

Mum leans over the counter, which is not too difficult because she's 73 and stooping comes naturally. "My daughter was over *Grigor*" – and she spits his name out like it's a rancid olive – "years ago. She's seeing a lovely young man now who comes from a very good family and he has wonderful prospects." And she pats the counter, like she's scored a point on a quiz show.

For the second time in as many minutes my face flushes and now the crooks of my elbows are sticky. My 73-year old mother is defending my choice of boyfriend. Soon she'll be saying the 24-year age difference between Seth and me is something to be cherished.

"Grigor is turning over a new leaf," Zebadie says, "and he's moving on. He'll be on parole in six months."

"*Parole?!*" says Mum.

Zebadie tilts her head and for a second I expect something to fall out of her ear. "The one thing the Plymouth Brethren Home Shopping Network has taught me," she says, "is Christian forgiveness. And pretty soon Grigor will have his Porsche out of the pawn garage and things will be good again."

Ah, so that's it, I think, as Zebadie turns around and heads for the door. She still wants the Porsche.

"Let's hope that while you're waiting for the Porsche," Mum calls after her, "the Plymouth Brethren Home Shopping Network teaches you some manners."

Zebadie smoothes her blouse over her breasts. And her eyes pop, like she's still surprised at their lack of contours. "I'm just the Messenger," she says. "But this is from me." And she points at my hair, the top half grey and brown and the bottom half faded orange. "Get your hair dyed again Morgana because you look like a bad drag queen! Ya cunt!"

We're having a cup of tea. As in, "Let's have a nice cup of tea," so it's Mum and me sitting at the table in the backroom. Mum sips tea from a fine china cup saying "Nothing like a nice cuppa" and "Good riddance to bad rubbish" and "I don't think the Plymouth Brethren Home Shopping Network knows what it's in for" and "She doesn't have the right-shaped head for a scarf, does she?" and "She does have a point about your hair colour though."

And I just sip tea.

Tingaling. The front doorbell rings again.

Turning her wrist to look at her watch, "That'll be the postie," Mum says, and putting her cup down on its saucer, she's through the door and saying "Thanks, postie," to the postman and back again, sipping from her fine china cup and a pile of mail sitting on the table between us.

And there's a large yellow envelope on top. *Morgana Malone, La Petite Fleurette Select Patisserie and Gifterie*, it says, in Seth's medical student scrawl.

Mum opens a drawer under the table and pulls out a letter opener, handing it to me. I slice the envelope open across one end and pull out a parchment.

Morgana Malone is written across the top.

And underneath that, *to be used for 12 Singing Lessons.*

Then *Marco Garibaldi School of Singing,* under that.

I shake my head. I don't know why –

"Maybe it's a present," Mum says, looking at me over the rim of her tea cup.

I stretch under the table for my handbag and dragging it out, reach in and pull out my mobile. And there on the screen, as I breathe in the smell of wheat flour and Demerara sugar and royal icing and wine-soaked sultanas and mock cream, is the tell-tale symbol of an unopened envelope.

It's from Seth.

I click the message open.

Can we meet tonight? We need to talk.

Letter to Q

by Gary Percesepe

Q,

I received your sweet email today and it made me cry. I have not been able to cry for a while (or write) so it was good to finally feel something.

But look – we are not very good with boundaries, you & I, are we?

I mean, we both know that I suck at keeping to established, agreed to boundaries, ground rules, whatever the hell we call them – but YOU – you suck too, it turns out.

I want to be honest here – I loved getting your three (count 'em, 3) emails since we agreed to have no contact. I love hearing from you, and knowing that you are thinking about me even as I am thinking about you. And this morning, in particular, as that magical hour approached, 9am–9:30, around the time we are always checking in with each other, getting caught up, encouraging one another in the new day, with the work – I felt a tug, a pull in your direction, and I KNEW you were thinking about me, and it was almost as if I was able to pull a response from you to my call, in my peculiar Aquarian Way, because – bam! – seconds later, there was your email today, at 9:37 am.

I love getting your emails, in spite of the fact that I explicitly asked you NOT to contact me, because it means that you are thinking about me, sure – but I also worry about it, because it demonstrates that we cannot keep boundaries, and this is not good news for you, or for me, or for your marriage. And when I am a healthy, fully functioning, generous, caring person (which I am NOT, these days – as I expected, I am having a VERY difficult time this week) – then I really really WANT for you to be safe and well and happy in your marriage, and not thinking about me.

Here is the problem: I somehow fell in love with you, and it was wrong and it is impossible and you are MARRIED with two young children, but it is too late – against my will I fell in love with you, and I had maybe two days of happiness but everything since has been torment and misery and terrible suffering and I cannot do this anymore. I just can't. I am in a very dark place, it is the worst time in my life that I can remember, and everything is falling apart around me. I cannot even count how many things in my life have gone terribly wrong, and I feel that I am making poor decisions, that I have some 'divorce brain syndrome' that just makes my mind lock up with grief and I say and do things that are inappropriate, and here is why I requested no contact with you this month: I DO NOT TRUST MYSELF AROUND YOU, AND I DO NOT WANT YOU OR ANYONE TO SEE ME THIS WAY!

I do wish I could get it back to the "friendship" stage – with laughter, much laughter – like we used to have, it was so fun, but I do not seem capable of that right now, and maybe never.

Love is a terrible, awful thing – it tears you to pieces.

I do not want to be torn to pieces. My life is a shambles and I cannot work. I cannot bear to think of the memoir – I want to delete it and throw my computer in the ocean. My novel is an unfinished, abandoned failure. I am half afraid of going to Amalfi because I have fantasies of flinging myself off the high cliff into the sea, my pockets stuffed with poems that will never be read – poems for you.

113

My life is like a scene out of *Moonstruck*. In one sense, it is really FUNNY. But who is laughing?

And there can be no happy ending for us. The boy does not get the girl.

I picture you reading this and shaking your pretty head and saying no no, and trying to argue me out of all this, telling me that the novel will be fine and the memoir will be fine, and JUST STOP THAT, but Q, you are so naïve – you don't really know anything about love, do you? Don't you think I WANT to stop feeling like this? Of course I do. Just tell me this: How does a person fall out of love? Just explain to me what the hell I am supposed to do with you, now?

Go on to another woman? Sure. Like Mary? We see how well that worked out.

Mary was the person who helped me the most when I was so fucked up that August day in Montauk, she told me that to keep the friendship with you I had to pour all my love and tenderness into the friendship and sublimate the rest. She was gentle with me, and she seemed to understand that I loved you first of all, and she accepted that. She was the ONE person on earth who SHOULD have been able to handle what she saw in the room that night.

And she couldn't handle it. She must have sensed something, she picked it up, it was electric. I have been trying to tell you this for months now. People feel it when they see us together, it cannot be hidden.

I think, in retrospect that Mary was REALLY hurt that night. I hurt her. I have to live with that truth. Just by showing up with you, just her seeing the two of us together, that hurt her. She responded inappropriately, of course, but she was upset and flustered and stuff just came out, and then later, when she had a day to think about it, and process what had happened, she just got her tail up and fucking stung me good, and warned me off her. And I have no desire now to ever contact her again.

114

What next? Go on to what you call "my androgynous poet?"

I laughed when I got that addled email from you about my "poet friend" who had contacted you and asked to be friends. And you asked me if I had suggested that she FB friend you. HA! As if.

Once I figured out you were talking about Rooney I was like – oh. So Q knows I am interested in this woman. But what does she know? Does she know I have not yet made a move to have her? Does she know I hesitate because of her, because of Q? Does she know that I hesitate because I want to prove to her, as I subconsciously and then consciously tried to prove with Mary, that, given a choice, I would choose her – choose Q, every time? And that it would be unfair to ANY woman, to be in relationship with them, because I would be unfaithful every day and every night of my life, with Q?

If I tried to be with Rooney, or with Mary, or with a thousand other women I might like or admire, Q – listen to me now – *I would still be searching for you in every woman.*

I would always seek to duplicate the connection that we had, that we have.

This is why I told you that with you something came to an end in me. I do not want to love again.

More importantly, I CANNOT ever love again. It is broken in me, that muscle. I simply cannot do it. This is it – I am going out on this one. There is a finality about it, a doomed sense of impossible love. No more. I have already told you this.

You tell me that this is untrue, you tell me that you really WANT me to move on to another woman, but I do not believe you. And even if I did, I cannot. It would not be fair to her.

I cannot be with another woman. At 9:30 in the morning I would feel what you feel – the urge to check in, to connect.

The only thing I can think to do is to disappear from the face of the earth.

To be in a place where you do not know where I am, or what I am doing. And where I have no dealing with you whatsoever. I don't want to see your emails, your FB messages, your tweets – they all cause me to suffer unbearably. I do not want to think about you or what you are doing or thinking or feeling. It tears me to pieces. I do not wish to be torn to pieces any longer.

Yesterday

Deep in the night I awakened with my new form of therapy, self-administered: I simply recite to myself out loud variations of this sentence:

I know Q loves me but she is married with two children

I know Q cares deeply about me but we cannot be together

I know Q adores me but she is a married woman, she has two young children

I know Q loves me, that is not in doubt – but we cannot be together so let it go, willya?

Q gives you all that she can give, it's just not our time, she told you that, so forget it.

Q, repeat, is married and has two young children at home, are you kidding?

Dude, it's not us, you said so yourself, Q cannot love you do not ask her to, let go let go

Today again

Ok – I was going to keep this letter going all month but I lost heart.

I can't go on, I'll go on.

g

The Clone Whores

by Nathaniel Tower

Samford has never been a one-woman kind of man, but he is longing for Sarah, the cloned girl with the tight ass he hasn't seen for a couple months. He hasn't thought of her much lately, mostly because he's been running from the government – or so he thinks.

Samford's burning desire has led him to a clone whorehouse called The Clone Whores. He wonders if this is some reference to a *Star Wars* movie he never saw. Samford fucking hates *Star Wars*. In fact, he thinks all science fiction is pure shit, especially the really dumb stories that have so little to do with science.

He doesn't know how he found The Clone Whores. Perhaps instinct has guided him here. He both hopes and doesn't hope he will find Sarah inside.

He knocks three times, as he was told to do. A woman in at least her late nineties opens the door and creaks, "You're welcome," out of her dying mouth.

"Are you a clone?" Samford asks, even though he knows it is too forward. He can't imagine the clones are really this old, but one never can tell. Truthfully, he doesn't understand how they clone the women at all. He learned a few weeks ago that men are cloned through sex. Watching himself birthed out of that blonde woman in the Motel 6 was quite the mindfuck. He also now knows that the man in bed with him that one morning was the by-product of his own reckless fornication with the brochure lady. He can't help but wonder how many Samfords are around.

"Yes," the woman whispers back.

Samford is not attracted to her at all, but her single croaked syllable elicits instant erection. He is a horny man, and he will happily fuck any clone that will have him. It's not just about the orgasm though. It's also the experimentation, and the knowing that another Samford won't surreptitiously emerge from the clone's vagina.

"Come in," the old woman beckons him. "There are many women waiting for you to mate with them."

"Mate?" Samford doesn't like the sound of this.

"Yes, mate."

"But I thought this was a house of clone whores."

The woman squeals with childish laughter, suddenly seeming half her age. "You have been misled, my boy." Her bony hand is suddenly resting on his penis, albeit through his pants and underwear. Even through the two layers, he feels about to come all over the skeletal hand.

"Do tell," Samford moans.

"The Cloning Whores are here to clone you more." She rubs her hand up and down with little passion, like she is dusting an old chest of drawers. It is the sexiest thing Samford has ever felt. His eyes start to roll back. The woman smiles. "My maker was a ferocious porn queen in the 70s."

Samford doesn't think he can take it anymore, but this isn't how he wants to go. He lifts her hand away from his crotch.

"You are a special woman," he says, "but I shouldn't be here."

"That's where you're wrong," she says. "You shouldn't be anywhere else. Come fuck my girls. They have been waiting for a man like you."

Samford doesn't want to go inside but does anyway. He is led into a giant room with a crystal chandelier as big as a hot air balloon. Only after admiring the chandelier and its sparkling beauty does he hear the moaning. He looks around the room and sees dozens of whores pounding away on top of men. They are all fornicating on chaise lounges, which Samford has always wanted. A quick scan tells him that none of the women are Sarah. Where the hell has she gone, and why does he suddenly want her so bad?

"You may take the open couch," the old woman says with a point.

As Samford walks toward the couch, he tries to divert his eyes. Although he is an avid lover of porn, especially the website www.clonedbitches.com, he doesn't want to watch these fuckers. But it's hard to look away when so much raging intercourse is happening right before one's eyes. Before he sits down, he spots a man who looks just like him. Then another. And another. Samford notices that every man in the room is his identical. The whorehouse is filled with Samford doppelgangers. One woman removes herself from a Samford-copy's penis. Within seconds, a new Samford bursts from between her legs. As if the birthing process has not even fazed her, the woman struts her naked body toward Samford's couch, leaving the new Samford squirming on the floor behind her.

"Take off your pants and give me your seed." Her voice is deep and horribly unsexy. Samford wants his penis to retreat deep inside his body, but it grows rapidly and bursts out of his pants, piercing through the thin fabric that hasn't been washed in weeks.

The woman does not engage in foreplay. There is no licking or kissing or petting. She mounts Samford's exposed dick and thrusts exactly seven times before he feels himself burst inside her. She is soon off him, and he leaps off the couch, not bothering to put his penis away before sprinting to the door.

"Come again," the old woman cackles as he heads out into the night. He looks back at her and flips the bird, his now flaccid penis still flopping about. She laughs harder, and he spots a woman who looks just like his lovely Sarah emerge at her side. It can't be, he thinks, but it is the only thought he is allowed to have before he collides with a body in his path. They fall to the ground together. Samford looks at the figure's face and sees the spitting image of his Sarah. He leans in to kiss her, but she doesn't taste like he remembers. He forces his mouth away from her and looks back at the other Sarah by the door. She is gone. Before Samford can protest, he realizes his cock has been inserted into the imposter Sarah, but he can't muster the strength for even a semi-erection.

"I'm all out," he tells her.

She spits in his face. "You humans aren't good for much, are you?"

Samford searches for a comeback as the Sarah pushes him away.

"What's your name?" he asks.

"Sarah," she says. "We are all named Sarah. Just as you are all named Sam."

"But my name is Samford," Samford protests.

The Sarah chuckles. "Keep telling yourself that, my boy."

Samford hears sirens. The police must be there to round up the clones. He slaps Sarah hard across the face and takes off running into the woods, his penis hardening just as he reaches full speed ahead.

Swallowed Whole

by Kimberlee Smith

She's breaking most of the rules. It's early, still dark, as Mum's hands hover over the Ouija Board. She's concentrating so hard to force a conjuring of what she wants to hear, that she's not allowing me to lead her. She's using the board, which was handed down to her by her mum, in the room where she and my bub will lay down their heads tonight. It's an open invitation to other spirits. Some that might not be quite as friendly as I am. Mum hasn't anyone except the bub there while she works the Ouija, and she knows there should be at least three people to manage the incoming spirit.

She doesn't ask me any questions. She's determined to control her own fate through the board, but I'm running interference and she's going to know it. She's been using the Ouija since she was a little girl – hid it from my daddy the whole sixteen years they were married, although I caught her using it now and then – so she has a false sense of security about it. It is not her friend.

Her eyelids are fluttering. She squints, peeks down at the parchment-color, stained board when the planchette slows and stops on *W*. There's supposed to be a person who writes down the message while Mum concentrates and keeps all fingertips on the planchette, but instead she lifts her right hand off and quickly scrawls the letter on a piece of scrap paper, then puts her fingers back on the black, heart-shaped disc.

I'm struggling with her. It feels like we're arm wrestling. Not literally going at it with phantom limbs, but spiritually, psychologically, emotionally. I'm going to win, because being in touch with letters, then words, then messages, is too great a desire I have to let her hopes take over when my energy can overtake her; I am certain of it. It takes nearly an hour for my complete message to get to her.

Waltz, Ma-til-da, home
Don't Tom Waits, make haste. We're all
Dead to Bro-ther Tom

My daughter Etheline, 8-and-a-half months old, claps her hands together and squeals, "Mummy!"

My mum, Maybell, sucks in a deep breath and all the color washes from her face.

"Now I know it's you, Melodie. Why won't you help me, darlin'?"

Mum puts her hands in her lap and weaves her fingers tightly together, like a church steeple. Then she unlaces them, picks up the gin bottle, swirls it around to check how much is left, which is never enough – the bottle is her only constant companion other than Etheline – and Mum fills her glass half-full. Liquid courage, I believe it's called. She reaches for Etheline's bottle of lime cordial, twists off the teat, and pours a splash in her drink.

"All I get is some cryptic, cheeky – what the heck was that message? A haiku? Five-seven-five. Our first communication and you're being *clever*? Tell me something nice, please, Melodie. Lord how we, how I, miss you." She wraps both her hands around her glass and lifts it to her lips, taking three gulps, and lowers it to where it nearly touches the table, but at the last second brings it back up to her lips for another swig.

I think the message I send is thoughtful, sentimental. We share a favorite song, albeit after my passing. *Waltzing*

Matilda. She discovered the Tom Waits rendition when she turned on the stereo in my old Jackaroo she's been driving on her cross-country trip to find my daddy.

Mum forgets to screw the teat back on Etheline's bottle. The bub squints her amber eyes and hisses long and slow. Serpentlike.

Mum twists the top back on the bottle.

"Baby, sometimes you scare the bejesus out of your sweet grandmum. I wish you wouldn't do that. If you have the ability to stop, please, please, do," says Mum as she locks eyes with the bub. Mum's are pleading; Etheline's are slitty, intense. Mum slides the bottle with all the premeditation of a well-conceived chess move toward Etheline, who snatches up the bottle while flickering her dry little tongue in anticipation. Her tongue is slightly forked. I watch her so closely so I am certain the split in her tongue is a very recent transfiguration.

I've paid Brother Tom, my daddy, and Mum's only husband, a visit, unbeknownst to him. Her curiosity bled over to me. I don't want her to see what I have. Brother Tom, founder of the Signs of Holiness Supreme Divinity Evangelical Church, has made himself a new home and a new family.

Brother Tom's aboriginal wife has conceived six babies. Five born, one every year, and one in utero. She's wobbling around off-balance like she swallowed a watermelon or two. Wait. She's pregnant with twins and doesn't know it. One of them is dead and she doesn't know that yet, either.

She has never been to a doctor and Brother Tom apparently prefers it that way. She's wearing a floral housecoat and a tight pair of mauve flats with bows, like the first pair of shoes she's ever worn in her life. A few of their littlies are running around with matted hair, in various states of undress. One is crawling; the fifth can't even crawl yet. It's an infant. The two youngest are naked. Not even wearing nappies. They all look like wombats. Dung-colored, thick, and bristly.

There is something up there in the Kununurra waterfalls that render some women very fertile. Brother Tom doesn't tell anyone, but I can see into his past and know he's brought his wife there over a dozen of times and forced her to swim in the freezing waterfall for the sake of procreation. For a man stuck to his religion, it's curious he would resort to mysticism outside his own to ensure she falls pregnant.

She looks bewildered and lost except for when she's by his side. He is the most rudimentary form of a Svengali. First he took Mum, who was only able to conceive me, then he took Alice – I believe she had a given name that sounds like the name of that band Kajagoogoo, but he renamed her Alice, as in Alice Springs. She is learning English slowly – he is succeeding in wiping out her aboriginal history and creating a new breed that more suits him.

Brother Tom doesn't know he has a granddaughter. Etheline's his first grandchild, and now I know she's not going to be his only.

Mum says *goodbye* (the golden rule of terminating a session with the spirit world), folds the Ouija board in half, places the planchette in a divot in the cardboard box just like it's a puzzle piece, puts the lid on the box, and stashes it away in her suitcase.

There are other pressing matters at hand and she wasn't keen on the message I sent.

I reckon she's going to ignore my advice. She settles the charge at the front desk, paying a spotty young bloke wearing a stiffly starched buttoned-up shirt with *Brolga Inn* stitched over his name. 'Tam,' it reads.

She puts the room key and a crumpled ball of bills on the counter and then smoothes them out with a flat palm.

"Checking out early, ma'am?" asks Tam.

"Apologies, Tam. We have a bit more driving to go before we reach our destination. Lovely spot. Sorry we aren't able to stay another night," says Mum nodding toward the bub, who's asleep with her head nestled in the crook of Mum's neck. So Mum did pay mind to the rule of not sleeping in the same room she uses the Ouija.

"Nice name, Tam. Reminds me of my favorite biscuits, you know, Tim Tams," says Mum, with a wink.

"Name's Tom. They made a mistake in the stitching. It's Tom," he says, shaking his head and looking at the squirrely stitching on his shirt.

"Ah. I see. *Tom*. Now, that's a good name as well. Good, solid name. Tom." Mum clears her throat and her face brightens. I can tell she's having foolish thoughts about Brother Tom. But I suppose there's no stopping her now.

She and the bub hit the road for a while and stop somewhere in the desert.

She realizes about a half-hour into the drive that she has no food left from her reserves and there're no shops around for kilometers as far as she knows. The lodge was only for sleeping, not offering provisions of any sort. She stops in the middle of nowhere and intuits there's a family of rock rats, which she senses are nearby in a crevice of a rock formation, and also picks up on a snake, a desert death adder, in the vicinity. Somehow she implores it to wind its way to the crevice to swallow the rock rats.

It obliges, swallowing three. I have a vision of Brother Tom swallowing his wife's aboriginal tribe whole. Without a single second thought, just pure second nature.

§

Mum has a slight trepidation in catching the snake, but of all the deadly serpents she's handled in her life, she never was bitten by even one. She's sensitive to them. She knows how to handle them.

After a while, the death adder, with a midsection distorted, bulging with the rock rats, slithers back out to bathe in the sun, but Mum grabs it right at its jaw with one hand. With the other, she takes one of her knives and slices it open as simply as if she were opening a brand-new suitcase. *Zip.* She reaches in and pulls out the flattened rock rats and plops them in a plastic bag. She shuffles around, eyes on the ground, picking up switches to use as skewers and then impales them, one rat to a switch. She cooks them over a tiny blue sterno.

The fur chars right off them. Those rock rats meet a similar end to what I believe Brother Tom deserves. If there's a Hell, and this is one time I hope there is, he's going to burn in it but good. For infinity.

Four Ounces, Plain

by Vanessa Weibler Paris

We're eating dinner when the phone rings. *Riiiing.* I look at Iris expectantly.

"You really want to get that? To interrupt our dinner?" she asks. "Really, James?"

Riiiing.

"Just this once?" I ask in my quiet voice. I can't even remember the last time the phone rang.

She sighs. "Fine."

Riiiing.

I push myself up from the table with effort. Tonight's dinner is poached chicken (four ounces, the size of a deck of cards, no larger, plain), broccoli (four ounces, steamed, plain) and iceberg salad (four ounces, chopped, plain). We're "slimming me down," as Iris says, for her next big art project. I spent my entire life being called "Slim Jim" and hating it. Now, Iris calls me nothing but "James," which I find myself hating even more. She has reduced me by a full syllable. By half.

Riiiing.

"What's the project about?" I'd asked, once or twice, but she covered my mouth, smiling, shook her head and stroked my jawbone with both hands.

"When will it start?" I'd tried a different tack. "Not until we reach two digits," she'd said. Two digits: 99 pounds. I'm not sure how close we are now; she blindfolds me for our nightly weigh-ins, which are followed by sex, blindfold still in place.

Riiiing.

Beside the phone, the flowers in the cheap-glass florist-shop vase are dead. Its card ("Get well soon, Jim! We miss you lots! xoxo, Linda, Barb & Dar"), perched on a plastic stick, is crumpled and stained, crooked, the ink smeared. I haven't been to work in weeks, a month, more. I have no energy. I'm not myself. I spend my days with Iris, dozing and talking. We move from bedroom to living room, as energy allows, and then back again.

Soon, I'll need a doctor's excuse or my work disability payments will stop. I should have sent them a thank-you note, the office ladies I used to lunch with every day. I should have called. "My cousin is a doctor somewhere in Canada," Iris had mumbled when I mentioned it. She was playing with her big box of shish kebab skewers again, wooden and pointy and ordered in bulk. Stacking, layering, arranging. "I'll have him write you an excuse for chronic fatigue syndrome. They can't disprove that."

Riiiing.

"Hello?" I say hoarsely, picking up the phone.

"Jim?" It's Bobby, my lifelong best friend. I haven't seen him in a while. Months. He got married earlier this year and that's what happens, right? When one friend gets married, and the other gets his first real girlfriend, who ends up moving in?

"Hi, Bobby," I say, trying not to sound out of breath. Bobby, Andy, Dougie and Jim: They used to call us the BADJers. Dougie even got us all BADJer t-shirts for Bobby's bachelor party. Dougie, who was diagnosed with testicular cancer the following week. He beat it, or so we thought. Bobby had left me a message a while back to let me know the bad news: it had returned. It was being treated. It was too soon to tell. But it'd be good, real good, if I could get in touch.

I should get in touch, I think. I should call. When I feel better, when I'm not so tired, I should call.

"It's Dougie," Bobby says in a voice that doesn't sound like Bobby at all. I wonder if there's something stuck in his throat, or if it's been so long I don't remember what he really sounds like. "Listen. It's not going to be long. You should come see him. He'd ... he wants to see you. You should come."

I should come.

I clutch at the counter. The vase crashes to the floor.

Eli and Damon

by Joanne Jagoda

Ah ... I've got to stretch. I hate writing up these detailed reports.

"Here is your coffee Mr. Dangott."

"Thanks Susan. This Starbucks Cappuccino is the best. I'm going to miss it when I head back to Israel."

"Anything else sir?"

"No thanks Susan. I'll be going downstairs to the interrogation room in a few minutes."

What an incredible view of the San Francisco skyline, but I wish I could share it with my beautiful Dafne. I'd love to show her this city. I hate to deceive her. Even though she may be a brilliant math professor, she thinks I'm an international businessman working in Silicon Valley. I'm ready to get out of this dangerous game, maybe have a couple of kids and become the businessman that I pretend to be.

There's my cell. "I'll be right down."

They're bringing Damon Southeby to the interrogation room on the second floor. I'll be doing the final debriefing, though Homeland Security got most of the details of the kidnap plot from him. He made a deal because he didn't want to spend the rest of his life in an American prison. Agents will be taking him back to Great Britain on the 10pm British Airways flight. He'll be under the scrutiny of

Scotland Yard, but his terrorist employers will be hunting him down like he has a bull's eye on his back.

He is sitting quietly, his handcuffs attached to bars on the table with his feet shackled. He's acting like he doesn't have a care in the world, humming to himself with a stupid smile on his face, but he's pale and I see perspiration stains under the armpits of his rather unglamorous prisoner tee shirt.

"Officer, we can be in here by ourselves. I'm not expecting any trouble from him."

I'm going to rattle him a bit and pull my chair up very close. I can smell his sweat. "So Damon. You're looking a bit out of sorts."

"Well you would be too, if you had shit to eat and you had to sleep on a three inch mattress."

"Sorry, this place isn't up to your usual standards. I'm Eli Dangott, agent for the Mossad. I have to tell you I found your plot rather ingenious. I'm tempted to ask you to come to work for us."

Damon stares hard at me. I flip through the binder that has the details of the plot. "I've read what you told the other interrogators. Uh … let's see … first you snared Anne through your phony website setting up a blind date who didn't show up. Then you bumped into her at the Fairmont Hotel, meeting her at the bar by accident, as David Lewis. I was in the lobby by the way, observing you. When she finally contacted you a month later, you started your whirlwind romance, including the glorious weekend in the Napa Valley. I trailed you there. You took advantage of her, you asshole."

Damon strains his hands against the manacles, glaring at me. His face reddens in anger. "I recognize you now. I knew I was being followed. You're pretty good at this game, Dangott."

"And I was parked in front of your apartment for weeks. We figured out you had to get close to Anne to kidnap one of the twins to be held for ransom so that the grandfather, George Donaldson, would give up his plans for Project Octopus. Surely you must have known that my country had a vested interest in this anti-missile system for our security."

Damon spits out his words. "They offered me a ton of money. It was always about the money, not allegiance to their cause. I was going to retire after this operation. I had it all planned." He looks away in disgust, as if he can see his dreams of relaxing with a tropical drink under a palm tree evaporate.

"I suppose you never got over your uh, working class roots. We know everything about you down to your expensive cologne and the size of your imported boots."

Damon's dark blue eyes turn hard. *I know I've hit a nerve.*

"We know how your mother struggled to manage five kids and ironed clothes to make money. How your father, a boiler–maker, drank his wages at the pub and knocked around you and your *mum*."

Damon's knee bobs up and down in an impatient rhythm. He snarls, "Well, so what arsehole. You did your homework."

"You were a brilliant student who got in to top schools on scholarship but never fit with the bluebloods. Then you got in trouble stealing lab equipment and computers and hooked up with the wrong element in jail."

"Has Anne asked for me?"

"Don't flatter yourself Damon. She hates your fucking guts. Let's focus on your operation. So you had your thugs, dressed as students, waiting at the Stanford Shopping Center. You picked up our agent Liat in the Apple store thinking she was Cassie."

Damon shakes his head, "She was a ringer for the girl."

"Yes, and you were rough on her, throwing her in the van, leaving her tied up on the cement floor, no food or water."

"I was ready to cut off her fingers one by one."

"You asshole, we wouldn't have let you touch her. She had transmitters hidden on her body and my team was close by."

"My people forced your Cassie double to call her mother at the mall instructing her to return home immediately and wait to hear from us. I made the ransom demand to Anne a half hour after she got home using a voice synthesizer. We weren't afraid to hurt her daughter to get what we wanted. She played her part well. She was hysterical when she called me saying she didn't know what to do. I had no idea she knew I was complicit."

"She was furious at you Damon. Go on ..."

"When I got to the house, I convinced her not to contact the FBI or police for Cassie's sake. She then called George relaying the ransom demands."

"And George was waiting by the phone with our agents who told him exactly what to say to Anne. He wanted to kill you with his bare hands. He supposedly called an emergency meeting of his top people. He told her he would have an answer in a few hours."

"I'll admit Dangott, I was pacing and jumping, waiting for his phone call. Robin stayed in her room. Anne was a basket case. Finally George Donaldson called and said someone from his company would have the specs delivered first thing in the morning. Anne convinced him that she trusted me, and I should be the one to take the plans to the drop site. I stayed overnight at the house. Anne locked herself and Robin in her bedroom."

"I was watching you with my cameras Damon, and Robin was giving me regular reports on her cell phone."

"That girl was always a little shit. Wait … you were the delivery guy who brought the plans. You had a Spanish accent."

"Si Senor."

"After you handed me three tubes of blueprints, binders of specs and a stack of computer discs, I left quickly, supposedly heading to the drop place but I took off for the airport. I had booked an 11am flight to London. I thought I was home free. After I got to the airport, I called Anne from the parking lot to say where Cassie was being held. I'm not a total bastard."

"My agents had already freed Liat and arrested the two punks who kidnapped her, but they didn't know what it was all about. We picked you up at the ticket counter of British Airways holding the tubes of plans and a carry-on with the rest."

Damon looks away and breathes resignedly. He looks at his hands attached to the table. "Now what? I've told you everything."

"Since you have provided us with the identity of who hired you, we are sending you back to London like we said. Scotland Yard will follow up with you."

"So I hear." Damon doesn't sound too concerned, but a line of sweat drips down his cheek.

"What will you do? You know your terrorist friends are going to hunt you down."

His voice is soft. "I'll disappear. I'm expert at that. And you might not believe this Dangott, but I could have really loved Anne. Tell her that for me, will you? She deserves better."

I'm surprised to hear the first sincere words from Damon Southeby's mouth. "I suppose I can do that, Damon."

I cross to the door and peer through the small glass window, signaling the agents. Two burly Homeland Security Agents enter and release Damon from the hand

and foot shackles. He rubs his wrists and shakes them out. They grab his arms and pull him to his feet, then one of the agents handcuffs his wrists together behind his back. They push him towards the door.

Damon turns and faces me. "I'm available if the Mossad is looking for *another* good agent." He chuckles as the guards push him through the door.

Authors

Rachel Ambrose is a twenty-something fiction writer from Connecticut. Her favorite season is winter, she enjoys well-made Manhattans, and she loves Southern fiction. Her work has appeared in *Crack the Spine*, *Exiles Literary Magazine*, and *The Colton Review*. Currently at work on her second novel, she blogs at http://victorywhiskeyjuliet.tumblr.com.

Lynn Beighley is a fiction writer stuck in a technical book writer's body. Her stories often involve deeply flawed characters and the unsatisfying meshing of the virtual and actual world. She has an MFA in Creative Writing and currently has 16 books published.

Margaret Bingel is just a writer, living in Manchester, New Hampshire. She spends her time working at her father's beer store, art modeling, and writing (when she can). She doesn't have a website or a blog yet, but who knows, maybe she'll have one in the future.

Guilie Castillo-Oriard is a Mexican writer currently exiled in the island of Curaçao. She misses Mexican food and Mexican *amabilidad*, but the laissez-faire attitude and the beaches of the Caribbean are fair exchange. Plus, the bounty of cultural diversity inspires great culture-clash fiction. Guilie is currently revising and editing her first novel. Her short stories have appeared in *Fiction 365*, *Lady Ink Magazine* and *Pure Slush*. She blogs at http://guilie-castillo-oriard.blogspot.com.

John Wentworth Chapin lives and writes in Baltimore, where he is too frequently starting Project B before finishing Project A. John writes non-fiction as well as fiction. Find him on the web at http://johnwentworthchapin.com.

James Claffey hails from County Westmeath, Ireland, and lives on an avocado ranch in Carpinteria, CA with his family. He is the author of a collection of short fiction, *Blood a Cold Blue*. His website can be found at http://jamesclaffey.com.

Gay Degani has published online and in print including *The Best of Every Day Fiction* editions and her own collection, *Pomegranate Stories*. She is the founder-editor emeritus of EDF's *Flash Fiction Chronicles*, a staff editor at *Smokelong Quarterly*, and blogs at *Words in Place* where a list of her work can be found. She's had two stories nominated for Pushcart consideration and won the eleventh Annual Glass Woman Prize for her flash piece, *Something about L.A.*

Michelle Elvy is an editor and writer who has meandered from the shores of the Chesapeake to New Zealand's Bay of Islands. Michelle has published poetry, short stories and non-fiction about travel, faraway places, food, motorcycling, slow travel, the kindness of strangers and raising children in unusual places for numerous literary journals and magazines in the US, Canada, Australasia, UK and Europe. She edits at *Flash Frontier: An Adventure in Short Fiction* and *Blue Five Notebook*. She can also be found regularly at *Awkword Paper Cut*. More about manuscript assessment and Michelle's take on editing and writing at http://michelleelvy.com.

Gloria Garfunkel is the daughter of two Auschwitz survivors which deeply affected her whole life and personality. She has a Ph.D. from Harvard University in Psychology and Social Relations, concentrating on Personality Development Studies. She was a psychotherapist for thirty years working with children, adults and families. She is currently retired, reading and writing to her heart's content. She has published many stories in journals and anthologies and hopes to eventually publish a collection of her flash fiction. Find more at her blog http://queruloussquirreldaily.blogspot.com/.

Teresa Burns Gunther has had fiction and non-fiction appear in numerous literary journals and most recently in *Northwind Magazine*, *Bookslut* and *Best New Writing 2012*. Teresa is the Editor of *The Lakeside*, an online literary magazine, and she founded Lakeshore Writers Workshop in Oakland, California where she leads creative writing workshops and classes and works one-on-one with writers. Find her work at http://www.teresaburnsgunther.com/.

Gill Hoffs lives with her family and an ever-dwindling supply of Nutella in the North of England. Find Gill on facebook or as @gillhoffs on twitter, email her a dirty joke at gillhoffs@hotmail.co.uk, or leave a clean comment at http://gillhoffs.wordpress.com/. *Wild: a collection* is out now from *Pure Slush Books*. Her non-fiction book *The Sinking of RMS Tayleur: the Lost Story of the Victorian Titanic* is also out now from Pen & Sword. (See her site or http://www.pen-and-sword.co.uk/ for details.) Feel free to send her chocolate.

Joanne Jagoda of Oakland, California, took an inspiring writing workshop after retiring in 2009, and launched on a long-postponed creative writing journey. Since discovering her passion for writing, she has worked non-stop on short stories, poetry and non-fiction. Her work has appeared in a number of e-zines and print anthologies, including *Pure Slush* and *Idea Gems Magazine*, and she was a poet of the month for a Jewish news weekly in Northern California. When not taking writing and poetry classes, Joanne enjoys being a writer-coach for ninth graders, Zumba, and visiting her three grandchildren in Jerusalem.

Len Kuntz is a writer from Washington State and an editor at the online literary magazine *Metazen*. His work appears widely in print and online. You can find more of his work at http://lenkuntz.blogspot.com.

Sally-Anne Macomber was born and raised in Toronto, Canada, and studied journalism at Concordia University in Montreal. Her work on high fashion and the demise of haute couture has appeared in various online and print publications in both Europe and North America. She turned to writing flash fiction in 2010, and hasn't looked back.

Jessica McHugh is an author of speculative fiction that spans the genre from horror and alternate history to epic fantasy. A member of the Horror Writers Association and a 2013 Pulp Ark nominee, she has devoted herself to novels, short stories, poetry, and playwriting. Jessica has had thirteen books published in five years, including the bestselling *Rabbits in the Garden*, *The Sky: The World* and the gritty coming-of-age thriller, *PINS*. More info on her speculations and publications can be found at http://www.jessicamchughbooks.com.

Gwendolyn Joyce Mintz is a fiction writer and aspiring photographer. Her work has appeared in various online and print publications. In other incarnations, Mintz is a writing instructor, a teddy bear maker and somebody's grandmother.

Mandy Nicol grew up in Melbourne, Australia and made a tree change to country Victoria in the mid-nineties – the decade, not her age. She has various animals including a flockette of pet sheep that are thankful for her vegaquarian habits. She writes short stories and loves flash fiction. *Pure Slush* is the first venue to publish her work.

Derek Osborne lives in eastern Pennsylvania. His work has appeared in *Boston Literary Magazine*, *Bartleby Snopes*, *Literary Orphans*, *The Linnet's Wings*, *Pure Slush* and many others. To read more visit http://gertrudesflat.blogspot.com, or email him at derekosborne1@gmail.com.

Vanessa Weibler Paris lives in Erie, Pa., with a guy, a girl, a boy, a bunny rabbit and a dog. She writes things both real (for work) and pretend (for fun). Her favorite things include hot peppers, bad puns, small-world stories, and tales with a twist at the end.

Gary Percesepe is Associate Editor at *New World Writing* (formerly *Mississippi Review*) and a Contributor at *The Nervous Breakdown*. Author of four books in philosophy, Percesepe's poetry, fiction, essays, and interviews have appeared in *Story Quarterly*, *N + 1*, *Salon*, *Mississippi Review*, *The Millions*, *Brevity*, *PANK*, *Metazen*, *The Brooklyner*, and other places. His collection of short stories, *Why I Did the Grocery Girl*, is forthcoming from Aqueous Books. His poetry collection *falling* and his flash fiction collection *itch* were published by *Pure Slush Books* in late 2013. He has taught at Saint Louis University, Wittenberg

University, and University of Dayton. He lives in Buffalo, New York.

Matt Potter is an Australian-born writer who keeps a part of his psyche in Berlin. Matt has been published in various places online, and he is, rather amazingly, also the founding editor of *Pure Slush*. You can find more of his work at his website: http://mattcpotter.webs.com/.

Darryl Price was born in Kentucky and educated at Thomas More College. A founding member of L. Jack Roth's Yellow Pages Poets, he has published dozens of chapbooks, and his poems have appeared in many journals. He currently edits *Olentangy Review* with his wife Melissa.

Stephen V. Ramey is an American author from New Castle, Pennsylvania. His work has appeared in many places, including *The Doctor TJ Eckleburg Review*, *The Journal of Compressed Creative Arts*, and *A Capella Zoo*. *Glass Animals*, his first collection of (very) short fiction is available from *Pure Slush Books*. Find him and more of his work at http://www.stephenvramey.com.

Shane Simmons is a self-confessed coffee shop writer who believes that regardless of quality, each paragraph penned should be rewarded with sweet treats (cake, muffins, Belgian waffles, etc). London-born, he ran away to Glasgow ten years ago, expanded his waistline and now blogs at http://scribblingsimmons.wordpress.com/.

Kimberlee Smith is a writer whose poetry, essays, fiction, and creative non-fiction have been published in numerous literary journals and anthologies. She was awarded a residency to the Jentel Arts Program in 2013. She lives with her two daughters, two dogs, three cats, two rabbits, and nine chooks on her farm in rural Connecticut. She received her MA in English from the University of Sydney, a certificate in the Creative Writing Program through UCLA, and her BA in Journalism from the University of Southern California. She is enrolled currently in post-graduate studies at Columbia University in New York. She can do a headstand on a trampoline, kill a chook, and make hard cider from the apples in her orchard.

Andrew Stancek was born in Bratislava and saw Russian tanks occupying his homeland. His dreams of circuses and ice cream, flying and lion-taming, miracle and romance have appeared recently in print in *LA Review*, *Windsor Review* and *New Sun Rising: Stories for Japan*. Among the many online publications featuring his work are *Every Day Fiction*, *Gemini Magazine* (Flash Fiction Contest Grand Prize Winner), *fwriction*, *r.kv.r.y. quarterly literary journal*, *Tin House*, *Flash Fiction* Chronicles, *The Linnet's Wings*, *Connotation Press*, *THIS Literary Magazine*, *LA Review*, *Windsor Review*, *Thrice Fiction Magazine*, *New Sun Rising*, and *Pure Slush*.

Susan Tepper is the author of four published books of fiction and a chapbook of poetry. Her most recent title *The Merrill Diaries* (*Pure Slush Books*, July 2013) is a Novel in Stories that follow a young woman's adventures in love and lust on two continents, spanning a decade. Tepper has received nine Pushcart nominations, and one for the Pulitzer Prize in fiction. You can visit her website here: http://www.susantepper.com.

Nathaniel Tower lives in the Twin Cities with his wife and daughter. After teaching high school English for nine years, he decided to pursue a career in writing / publishing / editing. His fiction has appeared in over two hundred online and print journals. His first collection of fiction, *Nagging Wives, Foolish Husbands*, was released in 2014 through *Martian Lit*. Nathaniel is the founding and managing editor of *Bartleby Snopes Literary Magazine and Press*. You can find out more about Nathaniel at http://nathanieltower.wordpress.com.

Townsend Walker lives in San Francisco. His stories have been published in over fifty literary journals and included in seven anthologies. One story won the SLO NightWriters story contest. Two were nominated for the PEN / O. Henry Award. Four were performed at the New Short Fiction Series in Hollywood. He is associate editor at *Grey Sparrow Journal*. During a career in finance he published three books, on foreign exchange, derivatives and portfolio management. Educated at Georgetown, NYU and Stanford, his website is at http://www.townsendwalker.com.

Michael Webb is continually surprised anyone is interested in what he has to say, and he blogs occasionally at http://innocentsaccidentshints.blogspot.com.

Other volumes in the *2014* series from Pure Slush

Visit the Pure Slush Store:
http://pureslush.webs.com/store.htm

June 2014 Vol. 6
ISBN: 978-1-925101-49-2

July 2014 Vol. 7
ISBN: 978-1-925101-37-9

August 2014 Vol. 8
ISBN: 978-1-925101-40-9

October 2014 Vol. 10
ISBN: 978-1-925101-50-8

November 2014 Vol. 11
ISBN: 978-1-925101-53-9

December 2014 Vol. 12
ISBN: 978-1-925101-56-0

www.ingramcontent.com/pod-product-compliance
Lightning Source LLC
Chambersburg PA
CBHW050822180626
46814CB00004B/1416